"Why d
like te...

Dinah's voice was a breathless whisper as she pulled her hand free from Joe's.

He shook his head. "I don't know, *señorita*. But I want you to tell me something now." He went on uneasily, "It's a hell of a thing to have to ask a woman in this day and age, but are you a virgin?"

Dinah stared at him. He was frowning as if the possibility was a problem.

"Why should it be any of your bloody business?" Her voice was trembly, and she found her hand touching her throat as if to still the emotions there. "What's it to you?"

He stared at her, his eyes cataloging information from her eyes, her voice. Finally he said quietly, "Because I'm planning to have an affair with you, Dinah."

VANESSA GRANT started writing her first romance at the age of twelve and hasn't forgotten the excitement of having a love story come to life on paper. After spending four years refitting the forty-six-foot yacht they live on, she and her husband, Brian, set sail with their teenage son to cruise south to Mexico along the North American west coast. Vanessa divides her time between her writing, sailing and exploring the harbors of the Pacific coast. She often works on her love stories on her portable computer while anchored in remote inlets. Vanessa says, "I believe in love and in happy endings."

Books by Vanessa Grant

HARLEQUIN PRESENTS

HARLEQUIN ROMANCE

VANESSA GRANT

so much for dreams

Harlequin Books

TORONTO • NEW YORK • LONDON
AMSTERDAM • PARIS • SYDNEY • HAMBURG
STOCKHOLM • ATHENS • TOKYO • MILAN

This book is dedicated to Joyce and Herm,
good companions for the long drive
down the Baja;
to Gloria,
who kindly let me use both her office
and her printer;
and to JoAnn,
who didn't get the letter until much later

Harlequin Presents first edition December 1990
ISBN 0-373-11322-6

Original hardcover edition published in 1990
by Mills & Boon Limited

CHAPTER ONE

DINAH had planned to get to Mexico in three days, but the driving was more tiring than she'd expected, and hotter. It took her four days from Vancouver to the Mexican border crossing at Tijuana.

By the time she was two hundred kilometres inside Mexico, the warm sun had turned unbearably hot. The country was beautiful, dry desert mountains covered with cacti, funny leafless trees she couldn't identify. The trouble was, she couldn't spare even a glance at them. Her relief at escaping the thick freeway traffic of southern California was quickly replaced by the tension of trying to drive a big car on a narrow, winding highway. She was getting to the point where she would kill for the chance to pull off into a rest area, but there were no rest areas.

Just before noon, halfway up a mountain with the sun beating down heavy and hot, she started the air-conditioning and wound up the windows. She was amazed to discover that the cooling system actually worked. She had bought the used Oldsmobile the summer before, had laughed when the salesman had said, 'It's got cruise control, and air-conditioning.'

'You expect me to pay extra for that?' She'd pushed her hands into her jeans pockets and told herself that there were other cars. If the salesman wanted top dollar for the Olds, it wasn't going to be her car.

He had said, 'It's a luxury car.'

'It's a gas guzzler,' she'd corrected. 'You can't sell these things to anyone these days.' She would never have bought a big car herself, except for the girls. For their camping trips she needed room for four people with tents and sleeping-bags and pots and pans. A Honda would never do the job!

The salesman had started to point out the cost of air-conditioning in a new car, and she'd said briskly, 'I need a good heater, not air-conditioning, and cruise control's ridiculous to drive three miles through Vancouver traffic to work. I'm a lot more interested in whether you'll replace that windscreen and knock five hundred off the price.'

They'd settled on the windscreen and three hundred off, and she'd had no cause to regret buying the Olds. She had had a good summer with it. It had been a good summer all around . . . her last with Leo. She had spent her work days concentrating on the new Madison advertising campaign, enjoying the artwork and feeling a warm glow when she saw her own work spread over the city on a big billboard. She had used her evenings to plan the camping trips and talk to Leo, her weekends to take the girls out and show them what the world was like outside the city.

A worthwhile summer, especially the time spent with the girls. Later, Leo had told her that Ellen had gone back to school and back to her counselling sessions, and she knew herself that Sally was keeping out of trouble.

Of course, the Olds didn't look as shiny after she had driven it through the bushes and up the mountains, but it was still comfortable and she loved the way it surged along the highway. As the salesman had said, it was a luxury car. Even nine years old and thoroughly battered, it still felt like a luxury car. As for the air-conditioning, she had never even turned it on—until today.

She passed a curve sign. If you could believe the sign, it was a square curve coming up, but in the last five hours of driving in Mexico she had learned three things about the roads: they were narrow, the curves were not banked, and the degree of the curve on the sign had little relation to the real thing. She lifted her foot off the accelerator and prepared for anything. The car slowed to a crawl. Beneath the roar of the air-conditioning she thought she heard a funny racing sound in the engine.

'I don't blame you, old lady,' she muttered as the curve started. This one was a false alarm, a gentle bend that twisted around a rock bluff. 'I'm a little tired of climbing mountains myself. If we find a rest area, let's pull off.'

As the car straightened out, she found another sign. *Curva peligrosa*. She had learned in the last few hours to take these particular signs very seriously. She had a Spanish-English phrase-book with her, but she had not needed to look that one up to realise that *peligrosa* meant dangerous! Those signs were invariably followed by a cliff-hanging corner on the side of a rockface, and once or twice she'd caught the glimpse of a cross on the side of the road. Commemorating someone who had died on the curve? She was a careful driver, but five or six *peligrosa* signs and one or two crosses were enough to make sure she kept her attention on the narrow road.

She crawled around the corner, then jerked the

car to the right as a big tractor-trailer rig appeared in front of her. She couldn't get any further over without taking a chance on that cliff, so she gritted her teeth and held her ground, muttering, 'Keep to your own bloody side of the road, truck.'

The truck gave way and they passed with only inches to spare. She was getting a pretty good sampling of trucks by now, and she'd decided that the shiny rigs stayed on their own side of the road, but the grubby, old ones took all the road they could get. This truck was the grubbiest she had seen all day.

If she ever made this trip again, she was going to take someone with her to share the driving and the tension. Not Warren. They had been dating for six months, and he had wanted them to take their holidays together and go to Hawaii. Dinah had been close to saying yes. With Leo gone the house was so empty, although sometimes his kids came and with their laughter and their problems it was hard to be lonely. But in the end there were always the nights alone in the house. She had begun to think that maybe Warren was what she wanted. At least he was stable, although she couldn't imagine how a person could want to earn a living doing other people's tax returns. Her own taxes were pretty straightforward, but she was always mailing her return just before midnight on the last day, and one of these years she would have to pay a penalty for late filing.

Yes, Warren was stable, but not dependable in the ways that counted. He had been hinting about marriage and Dinah had been avoiding the topic. She knew the Hawaii trip was something he'd been planning to try to get closer to her. She wasn't sure she wanted to have a physical relationship with him, and that alone should have told her that the whole affair was doomed.

It was when the letter had come that Warren had become history. A plea from Cathy, one of Leo's kids. The letter had been addressed to Leo. The envelope had been almost unreadable, torn and dingy and marred by tyre tracks. Tyre tracks? Had some postman gone berserk and dumped a bag of mail on the highway?

It bore Mexican stamps. The date on the postmark was covered with muddy tyre tracks, but on the note inside Cathy had written 'February 20'. The letter had arrived just over two months later, on April the twenty-eighth, exactly two months after Leo's death. Dinah had opened it because Leo had left everything to her, his insurance and his house. That last night in the hospital, he had left her his kids too.

'Dinah?' His whisper had been very strong, a contrast to his tired eyes.

'I'm here.' Of course she was there. Hadn't Leo been there for her when she'd needed it most?

'The kids.' The energy in his voice drained away suddenly. 'Sometimes one of them calls, or . . .'

'I know.' She had called once, years ago, and Leo had helped her turn her life into something strong and good. 'I'll look after them,' she'd promised as his eyes closed for the last time. 'I'll do whatever I can for them.'

Warren had thought she was crazy. Flying off to Mexico would have been bad enough, but with the collapse of one of the major Mexican airlines it wasn't possible to get a flight on short notice. The only way was to drive.

'Two thousand miles!' He'd come as close to losing

his cool as she had ever seen. She didn't suppose it helped that it had been two days before the year-end deadline, his busiest week of the year. He had taken Dinah out to a quiet restaurant for dinner, his only break that week. Putting down his fork, he'd pleaded, 'Don't you remember? Next week you and I are flying to Hawaii!'

She frowned as she negotiated another *curva peligrosa*. This road went up and up, was it ever going to come down? Why did the road have to go to the top of the blinking mountain? Why not go along the valley?

'You could come with me,' she'd suggested to Warren, her dinner forgotten. 'You know a bit of Spanish, don't you? You could help me find her.'

'For heaven's sake, it's not even *your* business! She's not your sister or your cousin. There's no relationship. If you're worried about her, call Foreign Affairs and tell them the girl's stranded in Mexico. I suppose someone will do something about it.'

She had felt something freezing inside her—the warmth that had been slowly growing for this man. She'd looked away from him, staring at a planter with something green and bushy growing in it. 'Foreign Affairs can't help me. What do you suppose they'll do? Contact the Mexican consulate about a girl named Cathy, last name unknown?'

She had searched Leo's records, had even contacted Sharon, a social worker who had worked with Leo. Sharon had checked the records, but there were too many girls named Cathy and no way to tell which one had skipped off to Mexico. Knowing Leo as Dinah did, she supposed that Cathy might not even have been on his case-load.

Warren wasn't going to help either. Rationally, she knew it was unfair to resent that. Leo's kids and the girls she worked with in her spare time were her affair. There was no reason why Warren should feel responsible for them. But those kids were part of Dinah's life. Any man she became involved with was going to have to accept that.

She pulled out of another *curva peligrosa*, wishing she could take time to actually *look* at those mountains. She thought they might soothe the psyche, and right now she needed soothing. Leo had taught her not to pretend to herself, and, looking at the winding road that seemed to go straight up, she admitted that she had known Warren would fail the test. How often had a man come close enough to touch just before she gave him a test he couldn't pass?

Warren had frowned at his baked salmon as she'd told him, 'I remember Cathy. She was at the house for a week last year. If she's asking for help right now, she needs it badly. She's not the kind of girl who can land on her feet in a strange country.'

Warren had sneered, 'And you are?' destroying the mild affection she had felt for him. 'You're going to go into a primitive country where they don't even speak your language and you're going to get by? You're crazy.' His jaw had firmed and she'd seen the muscles clenching as if he were grinding his teeth. 'I'm not going to let you do it.'

She had put down her coffee-cup and stood up. She'd been trembling, but she had not let it show. The woman at the next table had stared at her oddly as she'd told Warren, 'If you think you can stop me, then you don't know anything about me.' He had stared at her as if she were from another planet, and she hadn't wasted any more energy on him.

She'd cancelled her Hawaii flight, had a tune-up done on the car, packed a bag with jeans and T-shirts. Then she'd started driving on Monday morning, and now it seemed she would always be alone on this incredible highway. It was beautiful, yet frightening. She was half nervous and half excited by the way the road seemed determined to hit the sky. If someone would install a place to pull off the road every hour or so it might be a beautiful trip.

The climb wasn't quite so steep when she first saw the red light on her dashboard. 'Hot', it said, and the air-conditioning seemed to be faltering. And wasn't that steam she could smell? She had to stop, but there was simply no place to pull off the road. She kept on, slowly, crawling up the hill and hoping for at least a wide spot of gravel beside the road. There was nothing. There was room for two cars to pass, just barely, but there was rock on one side and the valley between two mountains on the other.

The noise in the engine was louder now, the engine pinging wildly when she stepped on the accelerator. She could see steam escaping from under the right front of the bonnet and knew she had to stop soon or there would be damage to the engine. She came up on the crest of a hill. There were more hills ahead, but here, on this rise, there was room for her to get the car halfway off the road. She hoped it was enough to get out of the way of any other vehicles. If one of those dingy, ill-mannered trucks turned up now her Oldsmobile could be wiped off the face of the map.

The engine quit as she braked. The only sound left was the roar of the air-conditioning, and she turned that off quickly. She didn't need a dead battery out here miles from anywhere. Before she'd started up the mountains there had been farms and villages, but now there was nothing but the occasional sign announcing a ranch. Ranch? It was hard to believe these cactus mountains could support even one cow.

She got out on the passenger side, away from the road. The heat hit her like a wall of fire and she slammed the car door in hopes of preserving the little bit of coolness from the air-conditioning. She could smell the steam when she got the bonnet open, steam and smoke rising from everywhere. She stepped back from the explosive sound of the water boiling inside her car.

'Well, old girl, I know we wanted to stop and look around, but this isn't exactly what I had in mind.' She pushed back her hair, feeling the dampness growing from the heat. Around her, the harsh beauty of the mountainous desert flowed everywhere. Majestic. Magic. Hot.

'You cool off and I'll have lunch,' she told the car. She had never had a vehicle overheat before, but the solution seemed obvious. Let it cool off. She would eat and then explore a little, then she'd start the car and go on.

She pushed aside a craving for a mountain stream with cool running water. She would love a cold drink, but her only option was a tin of warm soda from the car. She unbuttoned her shirt and let the slight breeze try to cool her skin while she wondered whether to take off her jeans or not. If someone drove past, they wouldn't be able to tell that she wasn't wearing brief shorts. On the other hand, if a motorist stopped to offer help she'd be caught in her pants and shirt. She wouldn't have believed denim could feel so stiflingly hot!

Joe managed to get everything into the duffel bag. He'd travelled light, knowing he would have to carry the heavy engine parts on the return trip. These days he always travelled light.

He took the trolley-bus to Tijuana, then crossed the border on foot and hitchhiked to the immigration station south of Ensenada, where he got his new tourist card validated. He had managed to get everything on his list while he was in San Diego. Once the parts were on the engine, he could provision up and take off. It was time to get moving again.

After the immigration station was the police check. He opened the pack and a guard with an M-16 pawed through it. He remembered another time, he and Julie flying into Mexico on their honeymoon. A thousand years ago, he thought, shaking the image away.

'*Yate en tránsito,*' he told the guard. A yacht passing through the country was supposed to be able to receive goods free of customs, but for a minute he'd thought the man with the M-16 might decide to enact some impromptu customs fee. *Mordida*, or bribery, wasn't as common in Mexico as it had been but, if a man with a big gun asked, Joe was prepared to hand over anything up to about thirty dollars. More than that and he would turn back and give it another try the next day with another man on duty.

His plan wasn't put to the test. The gun withdrew and he repacked his things. It was going to be a hot day, even hotter than the day he'd left La Paz last week. The heat didn't bother him much any more. He slung the duffel over his shoulder and walked out to the street, thrust his thumb out and scored almost at once.

A pick-up truck that had seen better days, the pick-up bed replaced with a tall, interlocking mess of wood, all painted red a year or so ago, pulled over. The driver was Mexican, a farmer possibly, and obviously friendly enough to stop and offer a ride.

'*Adónde, americano?*'

'La Paz,' Joe answered. The Mexican frowned, his straw hat shading his eyes. Joe said, '*Más o menos,*' because the truck probably wouldn't go all the way to La Paz. It was doubtful if it would get a hundred miles without breaking down. That was OK, too. He didn't mind turning to with a wrench to fix the engine and pay for the ride.

'Guerrero Negro,' the Mexican offered, and Joe swung into the truck. If they didn't break down, he'd be halfway to La Paz on one ride. He tentatively pushed his schedule ahead a day. Get the engine back together, provision at the military store, then sail out.

They jerked into gear, rolling along the farmland towards the mountains, the old truck shuddering every time they hit a pot-hole.

'*Cómo se llama?*' asked the Mexican.

'Joe.' The Mexican frowned and Joe knew he wasn't going to be able to pronounce the English name. 'José,' he said then, and the Mexican grinned. '*Y usted?*' he asked.

'Eduardo.'

Eduardo was driving his brother's truck to Guerrero Negro. The truck had been giving him troubles, but today it was behaving. He didn't speak any English, but Joe's Spanish was fluent, if ungrammatical. They talked until the road went up the mountains, then Joe shut up because he wanted Eduardo to concentrate on his driving. Eduardo was a frightening driver at best!

Joe closed his eyes and tried to pretend they were driving through a windy country road, without cliffs and mountains, tried to forget how Eduardo had almost taken them over the cliff on that last curve. He had only two choices: put up with Eduardo's driving, or get out and look for a new ride. Getting out seemed like too much trouble, and maybe it didn't matter all that much if he went over the cliff with Eduardo anyway.

The Mexican was whistling tunelessly, the note dipping every time they jerked their way around one of those mountain curves. Joe felt them turn a corner and pick up speed as if for the crest of a hill. Then he heard something and his eyes flew open. A car on their side of the road had stopped. Up ahead, a big camper just coming into sight was heading towards them. There wasn't room in between for Eduardo's truck!

Eduardo jumped on the brakes. Joe threw his hands in front of his face to protect himself, because sure as hell he would go through that windscreen! Eduardo didn't have seat-belts.

They came to a screaming halt about three inches behind the old car. Joe's heart resumed beating when he realised the camper was past them and they were all still alive.

'*El carro es roto*,' said Eduardo. The Spanish-speaking segment of Joe's brain didn't seem to be working. It took him a minute to play back the words and translate.

'Yeah,' he agreed finally, deciding that Eduardo had better nerves than Joe would ever hope to have. '*El carro* is probably *roto*,' he added, mixing his languages.

Eduardo was grinning as he slammed the truck into first gear and turned the ignition off. Surprised, Joe jerked into English. 'You're gonna park here on the road?'

Eduardo seemed to get the drift, but he just shrugged and said, '*La señorita*,' and stumbled down out of the truck.

Joe followed. He should have known! She was blonde, with long legs and shoulder-length hair. She was sitting on a rock near the car, had turned to watch Eduardo, and she was smiling. She didn't need to bother with the smile. Like most Mexicans, Eduardo was a pushover for a girl with blonde hair.

'Sorry,' she said, standing up and walking towards Eduardo. She had the open stride of a woman who walked a lot. No woman stranded in the middle of the Baja should sound so confident, but she was smiling and Eduardo might not know her words, but she was saying, 'It just quit, and I couldn't get it any further. I was hoping no one would hit it.' Eduardo grinned at her and she added, '*Buenos días*,' making the Mexican smile even wider.

Joe expected her to ask for help. He was prepared to be amused at her struggles with the language. She'd spoken two Spanish words so far and butchered them terribly. He was startled when she asked, 'Can you get your truck past OK?' then amused when she managed to get her question across with sign-language. Eduardo nodded vigorously and spewed out a stream of Spanish that had her blinking.

'*No comprendo.*' She mutilated those words, too, but she had a nice voice. Low-pitched. A little husky, as if the heat had given her a hoarse throat. She was perspiring, the moisture on her face a sultry sheen. Joe thought she'd had her blouse open when they came up. It was buttoned unevenly, as if she'd done it up too hurriedly. He was irritated with himself for being unable to get his eyes away from the gap where the buttoning process had gone awry. He could just see a glimpse of soft white flesh, and some crazy part of his mind was painting pictures of the parts he couldn't see, of her eyes closed and her lips parted on a sigh of pleasure.

Eduardo made another attempt, and she repeated, '*No comprendo.* Sorry. Just squeeze past and go on if you can.' She gestured to his truck, then the road.

Joe stepped forward, and said lazily, 'He's telling you that he can't leave a *señorita* stranded out here.'

Her head jerked and for the first time he saw her eyes, almost grey with just a hint of blue. They should have been relieved, softening with gratitude at finding another gringo. They weren't. They travelled down his long, shaggy form, over the jeans and the patches to the salt-stained leather sandals. Then back up, taking in the ragged T-shirt. She met his eyes then, and he had the crazy notion that if his mother could see him right now she would be looking at him just like that.

CHAPTER TWO

DINAH didn't see Joe until he spoke, but when she looked she recognised the type. A drifter. A drop-out. She'd seen a lot of them during the year she'd turned sixteen—hanging out on the beach, going nowhere, using summer sun, and a bit of begging to keep food in their bellies without much effort. She might have been one of them if it hadn't been for the clear vision of one frightening night. And Leo.

Her eyes sheered away from something uncomfortable in Joe's, but he didn't stop looking at her. His body hung relaxed as his eyes surveyed her lazily. It was a hard body, physically fit, but he had the eyes of a man who didn't get involved, who stayed back a few feet from life.

She didn't answer him, just let her eyes take him in. The T-shirt was badly worn, but it hugged the bulging muscles of his chest in a way that ... Maybe he worked out with weights. It had to be hard work that had developed those muscles, but she didn't think it was the kind of work anyone paid for. The jeans had been patched again and again, the patches sewn on by hand, and he didn't care who knew it.

His face ... She came to his face in the end, and that was when she realised how long the silence was growing. His hair might have been a light brown, but it had been bleached by the sun into a streaky blond. His skin was dark golden, probably as dark as it could ever get from the sun, nothing like the brown colour of the Mexican man's skin. He could use a haircut. Perhaps he cut his own hair once every few months. It had that look. The moustache was reddish-blond, and it was surprisingly tidy, emphasising a hardness around his mouth. He was clean-shaven except for the moustache, a detail that seemed strangely at odds with the rest of him.

And he was bored by this little incident. She frowned at him, then turned back to the Mexican. '*Gracias, señor*,' she tried. 'I'm fine. Just go on.' She waved her hand and he understood her well enough, although the other man had choked as if he thought her Spanish was the funniest thing he'd heard in a week.

The Mexican man looked friendly, a little worried, and he gestured and radiated the desire to please a lovely lady. Although she couldn't understand, Dinah found herself grinning at his assumption that she needed someone to look after her. Then she saw where the drifter was moving.

'Get the hell out of my car!'

He stopped with his hand on the driver's door to her Olds. 'I'm just taking a look,' he said reasonably.

'If I want help, I'll ask for it.' His eyes were blue, deep and hard. Hers were just as hard, but greyer. She thought their wills were about evenly matched, and it was her car. 'It's overheated. I'm just waiting for it to cool down.' He still didn't back off. He walked around to the front of the car, peering in under the open bonnet. She snapped, 'Don't touch anything!'

'I'd have to be crazy, wouldn't I?' he murmured, amused. 'The engine's almost red-hot.' He added a couple of sentences in Spanish and the Mexican joined him in front of the bonnet.

'Listen, just go on your way and leave me be.' She pushed in front of the Mexican and he immediately gave way for her to pass, murmuring something that sounded polite and incomprehensible. She reached both hands up and started pulling down on the big, spring-loaded bonnet, saying, 'It's fine, and there's nothing to be done but wait for it to cool off.'

She had got the bonnet down about six inches when his hand locked on it, holding it against her pressure. She stopped, her hands tight on the hot metal, her head refusing to turn to look at him. 'Does the Mexican speak any English?' she asked tightly.

'Not a word,' said the drifter. She could feel the body heat from him close behind her, could smell his masculine scent. With the sun beating down hard on her, his closeness had a strangely dizzying effect on her. His voice made her tremble, too. 'If you close that bonnet, it'll be forever before your rad cools down.'

Dinah let go and the bonnet pushed up, then she turned and faced him. Would his hands be like his voice, strong and sure, deep and almost shattering? Up close he was harder to face down. Six inches between them, maybe eight. The eyes weren't quite solid blue. They were flecked with gold. The face was hard, the jaw rigid, and he might be a drifter but he got his way when he wanted it.

She made her voice expressionless. 'I would like,' she said slowly, emphasising every word, 'for you to get the hell out of here. I know what the problem is. I'm dealing with it. I don't need some bloody American drop-out to come along and start tinkering with my engine for the good of his bloody ego. Get your hands off my car and get out of my life.' Her voice had quickened as she spoke and the

Mexican had stepped forward, talking rapidly.

The drifter said, 'I'm not American,' as if that was the only part of her conversation he had heard. The Mexican said something she couldn't begin to understand.

Dinah drew in a deep breath. Really, this was ridiculous, but the man would not go away. 'What's he saying?' she asked the drifter as his Mexican friend kept talking.

'He's offering you a ride.' Dark golden hands pushed their way into the pockets of those tattered jeans. She would have sworn there wasn't room for his hands. His body fitted the jeans so tightly.

She shifted, aware of her hot, sticky flesh under her own jeans. 'I don't need a ride.' She turned to the Mexican. He was grinning under his tattered straw hat, gesturing for her to climb into his truck. The truck looked incapable of going another five feet, much less miles and miles. 'No, thank you,' she said. He grinned wider. 'No. I do *not* need a ride!' Then, exasperated, she asked the man behind her, 'How do you say no in Spanish?'

He shrugged shoulders that were ridiculously broad. 'You said it. It's *no*, Spanish or English.' His laughter was the kind that came from a man who was watching a play. Did he ever get involved? Did he make love that way, his voice detached and his eyes cold?

She swallowed at her uncomfortable image, and said tightly, 'Tell him to go on, drive on. I don't want a ride.'

The broad shoulders shrugged. 'He's a Mexican. He sees a woman out here, car broken down, he's got to do something.'

She twisted her shoulders, followed his eyes, and saw that her blouse buttons were all fouled up. 'Why? Why can't he just leave me be? You'd leave me, wouldn't you?'

'In a flash,' he agreed, and she felt a spasm that was like pain. 'But he can't. It's that Latin *machismo*. You'd better take the ride. You're not going to get that car up this mountain. You've only just started.'

She hoped he was exaggerating. She'd already climbed halfway to the blue sky overhead. 'Just what do you suggest I do with my car? Push it over the bank?'

'You might as well.' He grinned, watching her fumble to straighten out the buttons. 'You've still got it wrong,' he told her hopefully. 'You're still one button off.'

She looked down and saw that the bottom of her shirt didn't match by about three inches. To hell with it! At least that gap was gone, the place where his eyes kept drifting. It bothered her that there wasn't even any warmth in his eyes when he watched her breasts. It made him a little frightening, more than a drifter. Inhuman.

She turned at the steady roar that was approaching from downhill. Lord! It was one of those massive tractor-trailer rigs. It was crawling up, letting out breaths as if it were panting. It came to a noisy halt with its bumper touching the dirty red truck that had stopped in the middle of the road. She looked back and saw the Mexican striding towards the big rig with his arms waving before his voice got started. As the driver of the truck started shouting in Spanish, Dinah saw that the drifter was leaning back against the side of her car, watching.

'Do you ever get involved?' Her voice was ridiculously irritated. She looked back at the Mexicans, who were standing in the middle of the highway, talking and waving their arms. There was a small car coming around the corner, downhill. It stopped just in front of the red truck. She murmured, 'Surely there's room for it to slip past them?'

'Probably.' He was standing straight now. She'd seen the tension snap into his body as she'd asked about him getting involved. He said wryly, 'The guy in the car just wants to be in on whatever's happening. If he drives past, he'll wonder what it was all about from here to Ensenada.'

'Oh, lord!' She looked at her car, at the collection of vehicles cluttering up the steep, miserable corner. 'At least nobody's going very fast when they get to that corner.'

'As long as no buses come along.' He was watching the red-truck Mexican wander towards them while shouting back over his shoulder in Spanish. He grinned and added lazily, 'As far as I can tell, Mexican bus-drivers don't slow down for anything. *Machismo* again, I suppose.'

Dinah couldn't help grinning, looking at this non-American with his muscular chest so well displayed under what was left of his T-shirt. The Mexican stopped in front of her, took off his straw hat and gestured towards the two trucks with it. '*Señorita*,' he said with a flourish. '*Allí está! El camión para usted*.'

'What?' She blinked. There were three Mexicans now, all men, all silent, waiting for something from her. Unwillingly, she looked to the drifter for help.

'He's offering you the big truck. Your chariot.'

'Offering me? You mean to ride in?'

'You got it.' The red-truck Mexican shot a stream of Spanish at the man who wasn't American. The drifter explained. 'He thinks you found his truck too old and dirty. He says you'll be fine in the big truck.'

'Oh, I don't believe this! I—— Oh, my God! There's a van coming up the hill!' The van was pulling a camper and the driver had already started his horn blaring.

'Not a Mexican,' observed her translator. 'He's too impatient.'

The Mexicans were talking among themselves, gesturing to her car. She looked back and saw there was still steam escaping the overflow container for the radiator, although that horrible boiling sound had stopped.

'Is there no end to this?' muttered Dinah to herself. 'We'll have the whole of Mexico stopped on this hill soon!'

'José!' called the driver of the red truck. The man beside her lifted his head at the sound, then strolled over to the Mexicans. So now she knew his name. They all stood in the middle of the road yammering away in Spanish. Dinah kept hearing references to the *señorita*.

The driver of the van got out and started shouting at them in English. Dinah leaned against the car, felt its heat burning her back. 'I don't believe this. This isn't real.' Surely that wasn't another car coming down the hill? It was! A Volkswagen Beetle filled with brown, young Mexican men. They piled out and joined the crowd in the middle of the highway. They looked like college students. She had a feeling that was exactly what they were, too.

One of the college students came towards her after a few minutes. 'Hello, *señorita*,' he greeted her. 'Speak Spanish?'

'No.' She smiled and he smiled back. 'Sorry, I just speak English.'

He grinned even wider and walked back to look at her licence plates. 'I speak little English,' he offered, his eyes admiring her. He asked, 'From Canada?' She nodded and he asked, 'Speak French?'

'A little,' she agreed. What Canadian didn't know a little French? She could lie in the bathtub and take a stab at translating the back of her shampoo bottle, although she probably couldn't carry on much of a conversation.

'We push the car,' he announced, grinning at her.

'Over the edge?' She jerked around, her hands firming on her hips, her body thrust between him and the car. 'Look, my car's fine. I don't *need* any help.' She closed her eyes and said desperately, 'Look, I'm grateful for the . . . the—I'm grateful, but could you just tell them all to go away?'

'All right,' said a rough voice. She turned and found herself staring into José's blue eyes, seeing again the flecks of gold. He was moving this time, heading right for the back of her car. She had thought he was talking to her, but he wasn't. He was waving an arm towards the Mexicans following him. Then his hand touched her shoulder and she jumped back. He said impatiently, 'Come on, *señorita*, get in the car.' He gestured to the college boy she'd been talking to. The boy ran up and pushed her bonnet down. Behind the car, a row of Mexicans were surrounding José.

'What are you doing?' He'd said she should push

it over the edge, but surely——? Her voice raised almost out of control. 'What on earth are you——? Get away from my car!'

José loomed up in front of her, much closer than an arm's reach now. He made her feel small. She was a tall girl, not used to being dwarfed. 'Just get in the bloody car,' he said impatiently. She saw the small car edging past the two trucks and the van. Behind it the Beetle was tailgating its way past. The road in front of her was clear now, empty. José said lazily, 'Before you stop the whole of the Baja from being able to travel, get behind your damned steering-wheel and try to keep from going over the bloody cliff.'

'Stop swearing at me!' She glared at him, but it was no use. She had no choice but to go along with whatever they had in mind. She might manage to beat José in a battle of wills, but she had a crowd of helpful Mexicans to contend with and they were immovable in their need to look after the *señorita*. She turned and opened her car door.

She said, 'All right,' but the resentment showed in her voice. She settled into the seat, then twisted to look back at him. 'Just tell me what you bunch of macho idiots are planning to do with my car. I'm sure *you* wouldn't mind pushing me over the cliff, but that can't be it or the Mexicans wouldn't be willing to help you.'

He grinned. For the first time she saw real amusement in his eyes. It unsettled something deep in her chest. She bit her lip.

He said, 'We're going to push this monster around the corner. You just sit there like a lady and provide the steering, and we'll act like a muscle-bound bunch of fools and push your *bomba* up the hill. There's a wide spot in the road just around the corner where *la bomba* can relax and cool off.'

'What's a *bomba?*'

'A bomb.' He pushed down on the bonnet to check that it was latched, and grinned at her through the windscreen. 'Mexican slang for a junker.'

'Junker? My car's not——' What was the point? She looked back at the crowd of men at the back of her car. They were grinning, watching. They didn't seem to be in any hurry, acting as if this were an amusing development to their day. Even the driver of the big tractor-trailer didn't act like a man on a schedule. She grinned and they all grinned back, every one of them. She would have had to be blind to miss the fact that she had seven pairs of Mexican male eyes following every move she made.

Beside her, a wry voice said, 'Mexican men are a pushover for a good-looking blonde *señorita.*' She met his eyes and they weren't admiring. His words might have been complimentary, but his voice was bored.

'But you're not?' She made it a question, although he was not going to answer. 'Are you a pushover for any woman?'

'No, so you're wasting your time.' He grinned at her flash of irritation and said, 'Let's get this show on the road, shall we?'

The driver of the van was back in his vehicle, sitting impatiently watching the performance. His horn blared. No one paid any attention.

'It's just as well,' said José as if he read her mind. He was a lot of things she actively disliked, but he had a voice that was deep and resonant, the voice of a man who should be doing something, taking charge of something.

'What's just as well?'

'The gringo.' He jerked his head towards the van. 'He's a prime candidate for angina. Overweight, out of shape. Smokes. I'll bet he has chest pains and won't stop eating red meat. If he joined in our little party he might just have a coronary while we're getting you up that hill.' He turned quickly and walked towards the back of the car.

She could have sworn that something had flashed in his eyes just as he'd turned away from her, as if he wished his words unspoken. She didn't know what kind of a look it was, but she would remember it. She might paint that look, that face, because there was so much hidden behind the lazy image he was projecting. Of course, she wouldn't be able to do a real portrait, not without him sitting for her. It would be done from memory, impressions of him rather than actual photographic details. It could be a powerful picture, capturing the mysterious essence of this stranger against the desert mountains.

He seemed to have taken charge back there. Funny, because it had been the Mexicans talking, planning, and him leaning back and watching with an amused detachment. Then, when the action started, it was his voice calling out instructions that no one questioned. What was it that made seven husky Mexicans follow the instructions of a tattered foreigner who looked as if he hadn't a nickel to his name?

'OK!' he called to her. 'Let's go. Put her in neutral and take the handbrake off. We'll take it slow and easy, up and around that corner.'

Very slow, she realised. There were eight of them, all muscular and tough except for the college boys, who seemed to have the enthusiasm to make up for a possible lack of hard muscle tissue. But the car was big, heavy, and the slope of the hill was such that she wasn't sure if they could really do it.

Slowly, it started moving. The right wheels crunched on gravel, then the front wheel regained the road.

'All right! Brake it!' It was José's voice, a bit breathless. She pushed hard on the brake, aware of the men behind and paranoid that the car would start rolling back, that someone would be crushed underneath and it would be her fault.

He led them all in a rhythm. Rest a few minutes, a bit of laughter and talking. Then the silence, the men in her rear-view mirror getting into position. Then his shout and the brake released, the car rolling slowly uphill under their efforts. Then his voice would call out to her, the tension of his pushing making it strained, breathless. When the brake was on, he said the word that had them all relaxing again. Then it would start again.

It took half an hour to move the car around the corner and up the slope to the place where it could be pushed off the road. Two more vehicles crowded into the traffic jam. She wasn't sure how many Mexicans were pushing by the time it ended. She was pretty sure by that time that her car must be cool enough to start driving again, but she was waiting until her audience had gone away before she tried the engine. She pushed it into park and put on the emergency brake, then got out and smiled at them all except for José.

'Thank you. *Gracias. Muchas gracias.*' It was almost all the Spanish she knew. They smiled back and the college boy looked as if he was ready to ask her to marry him. José must be right. It had to be that she was so blonde while they were so dark with their Latin handsomeness. She'd never received such an enthusiastic reaction from a group of men before.

There was another flurry of conversation. One of the Mexicans consulted José about something. José shrugged and looked bored. Then everyone started moving, the Mexican college student standing in front of her with adoring eyes and saying, 'You stay in Mexico long? I see you again?'

'Thank you for helping me.' She smiled, but shook her head and said, 'I'm not going to be here long. But thank you.' She thought he would have persisted, but one of the other boys shouted to him and he waved at her, said on a note of awe, 'Bye, girl,' and left her smiling as he ran down the hill towards the Beetle.

The cars and trucks started moving, some north and some southbound. There had been so many people, but within a couple of minutes there was only the old Oldsmobile, and Dinah standing and staring after the red truck as it led away a procession that included the big tractor-trailer and the van and camper.

José wasn't in the red truck. He was here, on the road, walking towards her car with a pack slung on his shoulder. As she turned, taking him in, he rolled the pack off his shoulder. It came to rest on the ground behind her boot.

'Got keys for this boot?'

She stared at him. 'What——?' She turned back. The red truck had gone now, even the camper behind the van had disappeared. The mountains were empty, and dry, the water sucked out by the hot sun. 'Why aren't you gone like the rest of them?' He was so damn nonchalant, standing there pushing the hair back and ignoring it when it flopped back down on his forehead. She could feel the moist trickle of perspiration running down between her breasts. How could he stand there as if the sun were nothing to him? 'I'm not giving you a ride. I don't pick up hitchhikers.'

'Bully for you.' He walked past her to the front of the car and peered inside. 'As for a ride, it'll be a bloody miracle if *la bomba* gives anyone a ride. You got any water?'

'Water?' She peered over his shoulder. 'I don't need water. See the reservoir? There's lots.'

'Dreamer.' He turned away and walked to where he had put his pack. 'I need a newspaper or a magazine.' She frowned at him and he said impatiently, 'A piece of cardboard. Surely you've got something like that in this junker?'

She was *not* going to react to his insults. He was the kind of man who probed and probed, hoping for a reaction. She was not giving it to him. She saw the boot swing up and ran back. 'Hey! What do you think——?'

'I asked you to open it.' He reached over and touched her chin with a dirty finger. She jerked back from him, and snapped her mouth closed. He bent down into the boot and said mildly, 'Keys were in the ignition.'

'I didn't say you could——' He didn't care. He was going to do what he wanted, ignoring her, smiling a bit if she complained about it. Short of picking up the jack and threatening him with it, she wasn't sure she could stop him.

He grabbed a sketch-pad that was in a cardboard box and she jerked forward. 'Hey, what are you going to do with that?'

'Open the rad. It can take the steam better than I can.' He stood up and she got both hands on the pad.

'You can't use this.' She held the pad tighter. 'Not my sketch-block. Cardboard, you said? Or newspaper?' She rummaged in the box with one hand and pulled out a Sunday edition of the *Vancouver Sun*. She kept her other hand tight on the pad. 'Will that do?'

He surrendered the pad and she pushed it back to safety in the box, then accused him, 'You got dirt all over it. Your hands are filthy.' She wished she didn't feel like a gadfly, following him, making silly noises. He was back at the bonnet now, pressing on the radiator cap with the newspaper, treating the rad like an explosive danger although it had been cooling down for quite a while now.

He said absently, 'My hands were clean until they started trying to push your car.'

The car was dusty. She looked at her hands, and they weren't very clean either. 'José, do you actually know what you're doing? Or are you just monkeying with my car for the joy of it?'

'I know what I'm doing. Stay back.'

He leaned against the wad of newspaper. She heard a hiss and he pushed harder as steam shot out on both sides. He was very still, seemed to push hard against the newspaper for a long time, and she had a vision of his arms weakening and his hard face becoming the brunt of a destructive blast of steam. She shuddered and hugged herself despite the heat.

'I thought so.' He was mumbling as he bent down. The radiator cap was off. 'You're almost out of water.'

Then he magically produced two gallon containers of water from behind the car.

'I can't be out of water.' She followed him, then followed him back. Her blouse caught her attention and she rebuttoned it while he was bent over the radiator slowly pouring water in. 'Where did the water come from?'

'The tractor-trailer. The driver left it for us.' She noted the 'us', frowned, but didn't comment. He added, 'But we've only got the two gallons. Let's hope it's enough for your thirsty beast.' He stopped pouring, watching heaven-knew-what in that little hole in the top of the rad. 'Must have been overheating for a long time,' he said finally. 'You got antifreeze in?'

'Anti——? It's not winter. What would I need antifreeze for?'

'Helps prevent it boiling. Must have boiled, pushing the water through into the overflow reservoir. Must have a bit of a leak in your rad cap, prevents the water sucking back in, lets air in.'

She was pretty good mechanically, but he was losing her. She almost asked him to explain, then stopped because it seemed like handing him a victory. 'If you thought it was short of water, why didn't you say so before you got the rad open?'

He leaned back on his heels, the almost empty gallon bottle hanging from the fingers of one hand. He was grinning. She was amazed to see that he looked self-conscious.

'I might have been wrong,' he said simply, shrugging away something unsaid, then admitting, 'I wouldn't want to stick my neck out and turn out to be wrong.'

She laughed. *'Machismo?'*

'Maybe,' he agreed. 'It's probably catching in this country. A man's got to keep his image up.'

She pushed her hair back, felt the dampness from the heat. She'd be a wilted flower before the day was over. 'I'll be glad to get the car started again, get the air-conditioning on.'

He frowned over her words and opened the second bottle. She wondered how much water that rad held. 'José, do you really expect me to give you a ride?'

His eyes lifted from the radiator and met hers. She could not read anything in the gold-flecked blue as he said, 'I'll pay my way looking after *la bomba*. I'm a fair mechanic.'

She believed him, but he was a disturbing man. The idea of sitting inside her car alone with him, going all those miles with his overwhelmingly masculine presence, was more than she thought she could take. And what was he doing bumming around Mexico, hitching rides that went nowhere? 'José, why couldn't the red truck take you any further?'

'I was elected.' He managed to pour half of the water into the little hole before it started to overflow. He lifted the jug away and she saw the ripple of his muscles through the thin cotton T-shirt. 'If I didn't stay with you, some of the Mexicans would have, they weren't going to leave you alone out here. When I suggested it, they agreed that it made sense for me to stay, since I'm a Canadian, too.'

She felt a jolt go through her, as if his coming from her country created an intimacy between them. She looked around at the empty desert, the hot sun. She licked her lips, and missed half of what he was saying.

'What?'

'Start the engine. Once the water starts circulating, I'll top it up from this bottle.'

She watched him through the window of the car, seeing bits of him around the bonnet. His hand. His shoulder. He stepped back and she saw all of him, and he was an impressive sight. He'd been perspiring and some of his hair was clinging to his face. His T-shirt was clinging, too, and any woman looking at him would have trouble avoiding a fantasy of him without the shirt . . . without the jeans. She grinned and decided that if he were to light a cigarette now the cameras could roll and the resulting advertisement would get a lot of non-smokers to go back to the noxious weed.

The bonnet slammed shut. She stayed behind the wheel, watching him, feeling the unbearable heat of the sun through the glass of the car windscreen. In the rear-view mirror she could see him go back, disappear behind the open boot. She felt the car shift as he moved something in the boot, then it slammed down. A second later he was beside her in the passenger seat, slamming the door, and she was glad it was a big, wide car. He was a couple of feet away, but even so there was a rather overpowering intimacy when that door slammed shut.

Maybe it really had been him in that ad she'd seen. It had been on that last camping trip. Sally had pulled the magazine out, and had flushed when Dinah had seen what it was. Sally had been old enough that no one could tell her what to read, but that resentful look had been an attempt to lump Dinah in with the other adults who had made Sally's life hell.

'Are those guys really worth looking at?' Dinah had

asked curiously, knowing she had to conceal her conservative desire to push the magazine into the fire.

'Some o' them.' Sally had grinned, and Dinah had found herself looking as Sally turned the pages.

'They look plastic,' she had said, and they did. To her it didn't seem sexy, the men posed with looks on their faces that said they knew they looked good. 'Except him. That one looks sexy to me.'

He'd had his clothes on, a work shirt and a leather jacket rumpled with hard use. He must have been working, his hair wild in the wind, and he'd stopped to light a cigarette. The camera had caught him in that instant and he'd looked up, his mouth closed around the cigarette with sensual firmness. He hadn't been the kind of man who took his clothes off for a camera, just for a woman, alone and with love. He'd been a man of action, stopped in the middle of working hard, and the sexiness had more to do with what was in his eyes, his face with the deep lines over the eyebrows, than in the perfection of his hard, muscular body.

'Do you smoke?' Dinah jerked when she realised it was her voice asking that question. But he did look a lot like the man in the ad. Funny how that picture had affected her. Her life was too busy for fantasising, but that night . . .

'No.' His voice was absent. He was examining the details of her dashboard, asking, 'Where's the temperature indicator?'

'Right there. A light comes on and it says "hot". Should I turn the engine off?' Her hand hovered at the key.

'Not yet. It's just a damned idiot light. Don't you have a temperature gauge?' She shook her head. 'Oh,

hell. OK. Turn it off and we'll give it a few minutes
before we start.'

He leaned his head back against the back of the
seat, eyes closed. He looked as if he might be
sleeping, dozing off, except that she could see the
tension around his mouth. He was a man who didn't
always have an easy time relaxing.

'Thanks, José.' She found it wasn't hard to say that.
'I wouldn't have realised the rad was low on water.'
She still didn't understand why the overflow had
water in it. Maybe she would get him to explain as
they drove. The thought startled her, because she
hadn't consciously decided to let him ride with her.

'It's Joe,' he said, not opening his eyes. 'It's just
that the Mexicans are more comfortable with José.'
He rolled his head on the back of the seat, reached
up and pushed his hair back. 'What about you?'

'What?'

'Your name, *señorita*.'

'Oh. It's Dinah.'

'How far are you going?'

'La Paz.' Her fingers curled on the steering-wheel.
She felt as if they were waiting for something, or
standing on the edge of a precipice. He was here in
her car. He was a mystery, a man capable of a lot
but apparently doing little, wandering around
Mexico with a big pack. 'What about you? Where
are you going?'

'La Paz, too.' He sat up, and said, 'Let's see if the
old car will do it, shall we? If all goes well, we might
make Guerrero Negro tonight.'

She started the car again. He was very still,
listening, his eyes narrowed like the man in the ad.
'Are you sure you never smoked?' she asked. 'Did

you ever work——?'

Absently, he said, 'I used to, years ago.' She didn't know if he meant working or smoking. 'OK,' he said briskly. 'It sounds OK. Let's roll, but take it slow on this hill. Let's not overwork her.' The wheels crunched, the car bouncing a little as they rolled on to the road. 'You could use new shocks.'

Smoking, she decided, and asked, 'Why did you quit smoking?'

'What's this? Twenty questions?' He looked ahead and shifted restlessly. He reached for his seat-belt and snapped it into place as she started the car rolling up the hill. 'I saw an autopsy done on an old man who died of lung cancer. Hey, don't turn on the air-conditioner!'

Her hand jerked back from the control. An autopsy? He must mean on film, a documentary. She started to reach back for the control that would send cool air into the cabin of the car. 'Are you a nut? It's roasting in here!'

'Don't use the air-conditioning when we're going uphill. She'll overheat for sure if you do that.'

With all the windows open, Dinah felt as if she were being buffeted around the car. She narrowed her eyes, hoping no dust would blow in and turn her contact lenses into instruments of torture. As they drove, Joe twisted around and adjusted the windows until they had a good airflow without quite so much violence. He told her to keep the car in low gear going up the hill. 'It'll stay cooler.'

'This car isn't used to having to stay cool,' she muttered, and he laughed. She liked his laugh. 'Joe, are you really Canadian? Where from?'

'Victoria.' He wasn't exactly a man of many words.

She let the silence flow over them and it was nice, glancing over and seeing him watching the mountains out of the window. A long time later he asked, 'How long have you been driving?'

She said, 'Seven years,' then realised what he meant and corrected, 'Four days. I left Vancouver on Monday. I—— Oh, damn! There's another one of those *peligrosa* things.' It took all her concentration to keep the car on track. She couldn't look at him, but had the feeling he was frowning again.

'There's a bit of a side-road at the top of the hill. On your left. Slow down and pull over.'

Pull over? Her eyes swept over the empty mountains and she felt the heat rising up from inside her. 'Why?' she demanded, and it was more of a gasp than a question. Out here, all alone, only his overwhelming maleness and——

'You're tired.' She glanced over, and he wasn't even looking at her as he said absently, 'I can drive for a while.'

It was too tempting to pass up. She spotted the side-road. It was really just a track. She got the car off the road and pushed the gearstick into park.

Without discussing it, they both got out of the car to exchange places. They passed in front of the bonnet ornament and she asked, 'You do have a driver's licence?'

'Yeah. A Mexican one.'

So it had been a long time since he'd been home. She wanted to ask, but his face was closed, forbidding intimacy. 'Why don't you go into the back seat and get some sleep?' he suggested.

Sleep, while someone else drove. It sounded like heaven.

CHAPTER THREE

JOE eased the car up over the last horrifying curve and on to the top of the mountain. In the back seat Dinah half sat up, vaguely alarmed, then sank back when she realised that they had gained a high, flat plateau. More empty, desert land. She could smell steam.

'Is the car overheating again?'

He didn't answer. Ahead, there was a shack by the side of the road. The car jolted as the wheels left the road and bumped over hard-packed dust. They came to a stop in front of a shack built from crooked sticks and old plywood. At the door to the shack, a woman in a long, colourless dress stood watching. Joe turned off the racing engine and swung the car door open.

He said, 'Let's see if she'll let us have some water.' He sauntered towards the shack, while Dinah sat up and tried to stop feeling like a sleepy, baked clam. If only she could take her jeans off and have a cold shower! Water! A cool drink of water would be heaven!

She saw then that he was carrying the plastic jug, holding it up to show the woman as he talked to her. Dinah stumbled out of the back seat and followed him, realising that he was after water for the car, not the people!

'I'm thirsty,' she muttered as she watched him crouch beside a big barrel. He had the jug immersed in a shallow cut-off barrel that was set up beside the big one. Between the two barrels was a plastic hose set up to syphon. Watching the water, her tongue slipped out to wet her lips.

Joe said curtly, 'Don't drink this water.'

'Why not? Isn't it good?' Despite the tattered jeans and the pack filled with what might be all his worldly goods, she believed he knew what he was doing. He was that kind of man. Dressed like a civilised being, he could probably conquer the world without firing a shot.

'It's hot.' He lifted an arm and rubbed sweat from his forehead. She envied him his balance, crouched sitting on his heels while he worked. He said, 'This water's hotter than your bath at home.'

He looked up. He saw everything. The way she had one hip thrust out, as if her legs were tired, her whole body tired. The way her thin cotton shirt clung to her damp, overheated body. The dust streaking her face. With the car windows open they were developing a coating of dust over their bodies and everything else in the car. He smiled oddly then, and she had a vision of him watching her as she sat soaking in a deliciously tepid bath. She hugged herself and found her bottom lip between her teeth.

She shook her hair back, stiffened her lips and stared at the water. 'I'm too thirsty to care if it's hot.' She tried to get her heart to stop beating so wildly. Was it this exotic, strange country that had her heart thundering and her mind painting images of a man and a woman alone?

'There's probably nothing wrong with the water.' He sounded as if the water were the last thing on his mind, and she had the conviction that he was having the same thoughts she was, although he managed to look as if he didn't care beans about anything. He stood up and walked to the car, and set the jug down. 'We'd better let the car cool off a bit. As for the water, most of the water on the Baja is good for drinking.' He jerked his head towards the shack. 'But her husband hauls the water in from lord knows where. She told me to go ahead, help myself, but it's obvious that every drop of it came in on a pick-up that probably isn't in any better condition than the one I was riding in earlier.'

'Oh.' Her thirst intensified with the knowledge that water was at a premium here. The woman at the shack was watching them and Dinah wished she could go over to her, talk to her and be friendly. 'I wish I knew some Spanish,' she muttered. She swallowed the dryness. 'If I was on a camping trip at home, there'd be a stream within a hundred feet or so.'

Joe walked over to the Mexican woman. Dinah had to admire the way he moved, the way his body spoke strength and grace and man without being all that obvious about it. She watched him talking to the woman, saw her smile and then laugh. Joe laughed too, then the woman opened a deep chest and Joe was handing her something that looked like money, then bringing Dinah a cold bottle of Coke.

She pressed the delicious cold bottle against her cheek, closing her eyes in a sensual joy at the coolness seeping into her face. 'Thank you, Joe. What do I owe you for it? Is that how they make a living out here? Selling pop?'

'Partly. She sells meals too. Hungry?'

'I—no, it's too hot.'

He nodded agreement. 'Before we go, we'll buy another pop. She deserves to make something off us. She's not going to take money for the water. You can buy the next one. Do you have any pesos?'

'Yes. I got some in San Diego. I've no idea what they're worth yet, though. The smallest I've got is a five-thousand bill.'

'That's worth about two bucks.' He had tipped his head back and sent a long stream of Coke down his throat. She found herself licking her lips and wondering if it wasn't time she got involved with a man again. Not Joe. He was just an attractive stranger, a drifter, a man who avoided closeness. She knew that about him instinctively, or perhaps because of that year before Leo had taken her in. She didn't need a man who was an emotional cripple. If she had anyone at all, it would be a man who could reach out and touch and love and give, a man who would stay.

She left him to fuss with the car, and went to the single palm tree that offered shade. Then she found herself involved in an exchange of smiles with the daughter of the woman from the shack. The little girl was very shy, but seemed fascinated by Dinah. Finally, after a very wide grin, the girl ran away and disappeared into the shack. By that time Joe had the radiator open and was feeding water into it.

'Can I help with that?' Dinah asked. He shook his head and she picked up his empty bottle and took the empties back to the woman. She managed to make herself understood with sign-language and felt a ridiculous victory when Joe looked surprised to see her coming back with two more of the soft drinks.

'Did you pay her?'

'Of course I paid her.' She opened her palm and showed a handful of big, chunky coins. 'I got about five pounds of change.'

He grinned. 'I take it you've never handled Mexican money before. Get back in the car. I'll settle up with her for the deposit on the bottles and we'll go on. We'll have to run the heater.' He rubbed his hands along the thighs of his jeans before he picked up the empty plastic jug. 'I'll get one more jug of water to take with us in case we need it again.'

'What did you say?'

'I said we'd take water——'

'The heater.' She stared at his hair. It was clinging damply to his head. He didn't show much sign of discomfort, but he was getting hot, just as she was. He might be suffering from heat stroke. 'You didn't really say that we were going to run the *heater*? In the car?' She giggled, then sobered because he looked serious.

He pushed his hair back and it stayed, held by the dampness of perspiration. 'If you want to get this car south, we've got to keep it cooler than we have been.'

She followed him to the barrel. 'You said the *heater*. You don't turn the heater on when it's a hundred and——'

'It's part of the same system.' He stood up with the water jug, tipping a little of the water into his hands and rubbing it over his face before he put the cap on the jug. 'The heater and the rad are connected together. Open up the heater, get more radiation, better cooling of the engine.' He sounded as if he were talking to a child, overly patient. 'Hopefully it'll be enough.'

'I don't believe it.' She got into the passenger seat.
He was heading for the driver's seat and she was not
about to fight for the right to drive. She didn't care
if she never negotiated another *curva peligrosa* in her
life! The door on his side slammed and she muttered,
'It's a hundred and twenty degrees outside and you're
talking about putting the heater on as if it were deep
winter in Canada.'

He grinned at her, his hands on the wheel. She
found herself looking at those hands. A small scar
on the baby finger nearest her. She couldn't see the
fingers of his left hand, but just a few minutes ago
she'd seen them plainly, had recognised the hint of
a depression on his ring finger. A wedding-ring, but
not any longer. Had he left some woman behind
when he went wandering?

He said, 'I thought they'd finished going metric
back in Canada. What's this hundred and twenty
business?'

She jerked her eyes away from his hands.
'Fahrenheit,' she said as she snapped on her
seat-belt, then stared at her jeans. She hated to think
he was right about the heater. She hated to think
there was a woman somewhere crying for him. 'I'm
metric on buying food, but for temperatures I'm
holding out. You wouldn't do this thing with the
heater just to make me miserable, would you?'

'No.' He seemed amused by her question.
'Actually, I'd guess it's only about ninety-five degrees
today. If you're hot, take off your jeans.'

He was peeling his T-shirt off, revealing a chest
that was even more muscular than she had
imagined, covered with a fine mat of curly light
brown hairs. She stared at the dark circle of a small,

male nipple almost buried in the surrounding hair.
She swallowed.

'Don't worry, I'm not about to take advantage if
you strip off.' There it was again, that deep husky
tone that was almost laughter. She swallowed
something hard in her throat, then lifted the pop
bottle and gulped a big mouthful of Coke. The liquid
had been out of the cooler only ten minutes, but had
already lost its iciness.

When she had confidence that she could speak,
she said, 'I'm not worried.' She wasn't, not exactly,
but she couldn't sit here in the seat beside him in
just her panties and her blouse, her legs bare and
her mind exposed every time he glanced at her. 'I'm
not all that hot,' she lied.

'You will be.' He reached for the air-conditioning
control and pushed it up, all the way to 'hot'.

It wasn't too bad at first. They ran along the flat
land, then down and down into a valley, the
windows open and warm, dry air buffeting them
from outside. Then they started to climb again. The
engine started that pinging sound, racing without
really developing power. Then the heat belched out
of the vents in the car, overwhelming the warm air
coming in the open windows.

In the next few hours she learned that an engine
got a lot hotter climbing *up* hills than going down.
When the engine heated, so did the inside of the car.
The air blasting her slowly returned to ordinary-hot
as they went downhill, then turned into a furnace
blast as they climbed.

She didn't complain, but when they went up the
second series of twisting mountains she undid her
seat-belt and drew her legs up on to the seat. That

got her away from the direct blast of hot air, but it wasn't enough. Finally, desperately hot, she twisted her way out of her jeans and threw them into the back seat. Joe didn't comment.

He was fighting his own battle. His right foot was directly in front of the heater vent beside the accelerator. After a while he changed feet, holding the pedal down awkwardly with his left foot while his right cooled. Experimentally, Dinah put her toes near the vent on her side, then jerked them back.

Joe laughed. 'Take my word for it. It's scorching.'

'You're not kidding.' She was barefoot. She thought she'd actually burned her big toe. She didn't wonder any longer why Joe kept changing feet on the accelerator, didn't comment about the lurch the car gave when his feet shifted.

The silence seemed more comfortable. She thought she had regained her equilibrium. She actually managed to look over at him without letting her eyes travel down over his bare chest to the play of muscles across his midriff. Maybe looking at that magazine with Sally had done something to her! Whatever it was, she had it under control now. She felt relaxed, almost enjoying sharing the heat and the mountains with him.

His voice interrupted the silence first. 'Your first trip down here? Yes, of course it is. You don't know the money, don't know the language.'

She nodded, but he didn't see. His eyes were on the road and she said fancifully, 'Maybe I'll become a snowbird.' She looked at the way the blue sky met the green mountains. From this far away, it looked like there were trees on the mountains. From what she had seen so far, it was probably cacti. 'I'll spend the summers in Canada, my winters down here. I bet it never freezes here. And it doesn't rain much, does it? This land hasn't seen water in a long time.'

He shifted his shoulders. He had a relaxed style of driving that was very expert. 'Lots of people play the snowbird routine. Here in winters, north in summers.'

'Not for me,' she said, lying her arm on the open window to deflect more of the outside air towards herself. 'That's just an idle fantasy. Wandering is for holidays. A person needs a home. Without my home, I'd be nothing, nobody.' He glanced at her and she realised how intensely personal that comment had been. She turned away, looked out of the window, and asked abruptly, 'What kind of cows are those?'

There had been quite a variety in the colour of the cows that grazed among the cacti. Most of them seemed to be unfenced, although Joe hadn't had to swerve to avoid one on the road yet.

'Beef cow,' he said now.

She closed her eyes and tried not to see him. 'Do you know that you talk in shorthand? No extra ands and buts, no picturesque adjectives. You sound like someone communicating by two-way radio, trying to get the information as succinctly as possible.'

'Probably.' He grinned too, hearing the brevity of his answer. 'I do talk on radio, sometimes more than I talk in person.'

They drove in silence for five minutes before Dinah gave up waiting for him to explain and asked, 'Why? Why do you meet more people on radio than in person?'

'I've got a sailboat down at La Paz. I've been cruising around. Sometimes it's a lot of miles between people.'

His eyes raked over her scantily dressed body and she felt suddenly aware of how white her legs were, how thin the cotton shirt, how silky the fabric of her underwear. Thank God that at least she was wearing a bra! She pulled on the shirt, trying to get it away from its clinging grip on her flesh.

'Don't worry about it,' he said, his eyes on the road again. 'People have to dress lightly in this weather.' She found her eyes following his naked torso to where his belt dug into the flesh above his waist. When he moved the steering-wheel, she could see the muscles ripple all down his naked front. Then his voice lost the laziness, became deliberate. 'I'm your opposite number, Dinah. I'm not even a snowbird because I stay in the latitudes where there's never snow. When things get uncomfortable, too hot or too cold, or even too complicated—I move on.'

It was a warning—a kind warning, she supposed. She was aware of him, and he was aware of her, too. He was telling her that he wasn't the kind of man she should set her sights on. She said carefully, 'I knew that.' Her voice was only a whisper and she tried to strengthen it. 'I didn't know about the hot and the cold, but when you walked up to me back there—when you walked out from behind that Mexican in the red truck . . . I knew you were a man who always moved on before the roots started growing.'

'Not always.' Something crossed his face and she knew that the wife and children she had fantasised weren't waiting at home, crying for him. Whatever had happened, it had hurt him, left him alone, perhaps driven him out on this crazy rambling life.

Her lips were parted, but the rigid line of his mouth forbade those kinds of questions. 'Have you been in Mexico long?' she asked instead. 'Can you tell me about these mountains? Some of them look like hard rock, others are just a heap of gravel, but there's nowhere it could have come from.'

The tension eased as he told her about the land they were travelling over, the names of the cacti and the way some of the land had been formed by volcanic action and some by glaciers from a bygone ice age.

'Some of it's sedimentary, too,' he told her, becoming more enthusiastic as he realised she really was interested. 'See that slope over there? You can see the layering from sedimentary deposits. At one time all of this was underwater, the ocean floor.'

'I could go for a bit of ocean right now,' she said wryly.

'A swim?' He was smiling as if the idea appealed to him, too.

'Yeah.' She wiggled her toes, shifting them to get away from that horrible hot air. 'It sounds like heaven.'

Heaven was when they came on to a flat plateau that went for miles and miles, and Joe decreed that they could turn the heater off. The hottest part of the day was over, the sun about to set, and the car could take it easy along the flat.

'Better look for a hotel,' he said, as the rosy glow grew in the sky.

'We can drive all night.' She twisted her shoulders to ease the tension. 'I slept earlier. You can bed down in the back while I drive.'

'No.' He slowed down and eased the car between

two big cows that had appeared out of nowhere. 'We'll find a hotel. There'll be something reasonable in the next village. It's a fair size.'

'But——' Why was she letting him take over the decisions? Where to get water. Turning on the heater. Now the hotel. 'Joe, I want to drive all night. It's my——'

'You'll hit a cow. Or a bus.' He pulled off the road, turned, and they were bumping along a gravel road towards a small settlement. 'You've seen enough livestock to know the cows run loose in this country, and at night how are you going to spot them? I can tell you that you won't always find them in your headlights in time to avoid hitting them. If that's not bad enough, the buses roar along these highways at night at a terrible rate. They know damned well there's no one else on the roads after dark and they don't mind taking up the whole road.'

He stopped outside a sprawling building. They'd found some kind of town, or at least a scattering of buildings. Joe turned the key and everything was quiet, the wind gone, the sounds of laughter coming over the air from somewhere nearby.

He said flatly, 'Nobody travels at night on the Baja. Nobody sane. It's suicide.'

She thought of the buses, of the *curvas peligrosas*. She shuddered, knowing that you only had to add a cow or two and she could easily find herself at the bottom of one of those cliffs.

'Is this a hotel?' It looked a bit like one, although she couldn't see a sign. She wondered if a room would have a shower. If she couldn't jump in the ocean, a shower would be a heavenly alternative.

He leaned back in the driver's seat and released

his seat-belt. The belt disturbed the mat of his chest hair as it retracted. He turned and retrieved his shirt from the back seat. She told herself she was glad to see his broad, naked chest covered.

He said, 'A reasonable hotel. Comfortable enough, not expensive.' He twisted his shoulders, settled the shirt down over his chest. 'Get yourself a room for the night. I'll sleep in the car.'

Why? Had she misjudged him? A drifter, but she hadn't thought he would do anything like steal her car or hit her over the head or rape her in the middle of nowhere.

He had leaned back and closed his eyes. She tried to see something in the lines of his face. 'Joe, do they speak English in there?'

'I doubt it.' He grinned, the eyelids remaining closed. She saw him shift his shoulders as if they were stiff from all the driving.

She bit out angrily, 'I don't know how to ask for a hotel room in Spanish.' What was the word for room? Right now she felt too exhausted to deal with sign-language and strange-sounding words. He was quiet, still. She saw his fingers curl around the steering-wheel. 'Joe?'

His words were very deliberately harsh. 'Lady, I'm not your baby-sitter. You came down here alone for some crazy reason. If you don't know the language you should take a plane, book a tour or something. You don't go driving through the frontier of Baja alone when you don't have a clue about anything.'

He opened the door and unfolded himself, stretching as he stood. Then he slammed the door and walked away, not looking back, going heaven knew where. And, damn it! He had her car keys!

Did he expect her to chase after him, pleading and acting like the dizzy blonde female he seemed to have decided she was?

She wouldn't do it. She really didn't care very much whether he took the car or not. She was not capable of the energy required to go after him. Lucky he hadn't given in when she'd suggested driving all night. She felt as if a steamroller had hit her, or a blast furnace. Right now the idea of a shower and a real bed took precedence over everything else.

She got out and locked the car door. Then she detached the little magnetic holder with her spare keys in it from under the front bumper and got her suitcase out of the boot. Spanish or not, she would get herself a room.

Actually, it was easier than she had thought. The man she found in the office did not speak English, but within ten minutes she was inside a very plain, very clean room with two hard beds. She tried both beds, and decided the wider one was more comfortable.

She had her suitcase open on the narrower bed and was unpacking the necessities for a wash in the tiny bathroom when someone knocked on the door. What was it about that brief rapping that reminded her of Joe? No wasted motion. No extra sounds. She opened the door.

He wasn't leaning against the door-jamb, but he looked tired, as if he wanted to. His face was tense, strained. He smiled at her, but it was a weak effort. He seemed almost nervous as he pushed his hair back. It seemed he wasn't going to talk, just stand there.

'Hi,' said Dinah

He grimaced and said, 'Look, I'm sorry.'

She frowned at him, but he looked terribly tired. She didn't know why that should touch her somewhere near her heart, but she felt soft and weak, had to fight an overwhelming urge to touch his cheek, to smooth the disturbed lines from his forehead.

She made herself shrug, made her voice in different. 'I did all right without you. I got a room.'

She turned away. He might as well come in. A car in the middle of nowhere or a hotel room. It didn't seem to make much difference. This hotel room was very bare and not at all romantic. She walked across and sat down beside her suitcase.

He didn't comment on her accomplishment in getting a room without him. She had felt proud of managing to communicate without the help of a common language. Now it seemed a trivial victory. 'The man knew I wanted a room. After all, if you run a hotel and some woman comes through the door with a suitcase, you're not going to try to sell her a stereo, are you?'

He didn't say anything.

She said dully, 'We even managed to communicate about the money.' Why didn't he talk? Not that he was a chatty man, but up until now he'd been willing to at least say the odd word. 'I'm not helpless, you know. I didn't ask you to help me. It was your idea, and those Mexicans. I'd have done fine on my own.'

Would she? The car had needed water, and it would have taken her a long time to figure that out with the overflow reservoir full. Where would she have found water in the desert?

He didn't close the door. She thought he didn't even realise it was open. He said, 'Of course you're not helpless.'

His eyes were on the empty bed like the eyes of a man dreaming about heaven. Why hadn't he wanted to take a hotel room? Was he that short of money? He might be. He'd been hitching rides, and hadn't she heard that travelling by bus in Mexico was incredibly cheap? So he hadn't been able to afford a bus.

'Does the room have a shower?' he asked.

'Yes, but there aren't any towels.' She'd been dreaming about a shower, had been trying to find out how to ask for towels in her phrase-book when he'd knocked on the door.

'They don't usually put them in the rooms.' He rubbed the back of his hand across his eyes. 'You have to ask. I'll get them for you.' She opened her lips to protest and he said in a low voice, 'I was having a fit of temper, OK. I know you're not helpless, and I'm sure you'd get yourself from here to Timbuktu in one piece if you decided you wanted to.'

She found her eyes caught in his. How did he know that? Most men assumed she wanted to be looked after, like Warren with his ridiculous conviction that she couldn't travel without a man. Joe looked at her as if he knew her all the way through. Was she transparent to him? Was it an illusion, the feeling that she knew him from some other time, some other life?

'I have to get to La Paz,' she said quietly. 'It's not just a vacation. Somebody needs my help, and I had to come.'

He drew in a deep breath, seemed ready to say something, then swallowed the words. He muttered something in Spanish as he turned around and started walking out of the room.

'Where are you going now?' She followed him to the door. 'Why are you leaving?' So, all right, he left when complications developed, but she'd like someone to show her a complication. She had been getting ready to ask his advice on how to find Cathy. He seemed to know the ropes in this country, and she had known all along that she would need to find someone to help her. She wasn't going to ask for active help, just *advice*, for heaven's sake!

But there was only his back, walking away across the courtyard towards the road. 'Joe?' He stopped, didn't look back, and her voice was more weary than she realised when she asked, 'Do you ever stick around to finish off a conversation? You took off in the car when we—and now—'

Damn! He was walking on. He was walking away, might never come back for all she knew. It shouldn't matter. He was nothing, nobody. A drifter. Not a man she should ever think about, and definitely not one that seemed to want to think about her. She slammed the door that he hadn't bothered to close and rummaged in her suitcase for the face-cloth and hand towel she thought she might have packed.

But part of her understood. She didn't know how he had been hurt, what he was running from, but she knew about running. She remembered that day, ten years ago, the day she had stopped running. Standing in Leo's living-room after he had driven her to his house, she'd swung on him.

'I don't need anyone. I don't need you. I don't need

anywhere. I bloody don't want any more damned family life! You gave me your number and I just thought I'd call and say hello.' She'd swallowed fear of the outside and gritted, 'So I said hello, and now I'm going.'

Luckily she hadn't really walked back out of that door, because that night her life had turned from running into building, but she still understood about running. Maybe that was why Joe bothered her so much. He would have his own story, his own reasons for the closed look on his face. But the feelings were the same. She had been running, she supposed, where Joe seemed to be just rambling, but it came to the same thing. But she'd had the sense to stop and reach for someone who could help. Joe could be out there on his boat, alone, a hundred years from now.

She locked the door that she had closed, shutting him out of her mind. She had no room for anyone but Cathy right now.

The hot water was not exactly hot. It ran tepid and not very plentiful. She pulled the skimpy shower curtain and stood under the water, soaping herself and rinsing off the dust and sweat slowly, twisting this way and that to get the water on the right places. She hadn't been able to find her shampoo in the suitcase; she must have left it in the hotel back in San Diego. She washed her hair using bar soap, needing to feel it clean and smooth before she slept.

She slicked the moisture off her body with her hands, hoping that she could get reasonably dry with one small hand towel. If not, she was sure she would air-dry in minutes. It was so warm. She pushed the curtain aside and——

There were two bath towels folded on the edge of the bathroom sink. She craned her head around the curtain. The bathroom door was closed. She hadn't closed it. There hadn't seemed any need when she was alone in the locked hotel room.

She padded across the bathroom floor in her wet feet, reaching for the door in case there was someone out there still, someone who might walk in on her. But there was no lock, only an ordinary latch. And someone had already walked in, had put the towels on the sink and closed the door. She picked up a towel and wrapped her hair in it, then started rubbing her skin dry with the other towel. The hotel man? Surely he wouldn't walk right into the bathroom when she was showering? Wouldn't he knock?

Was there someone out there?

She held the towel in front of her. It was thin and small for a bath towel. It could not possibly cover both her front and back at the same time. She held it as best she could and opened the door a crack.

'Is there someone out there?'

Silence. She strained her ears. The sound of music from somewhere outside. A sound that might be the ocean somewhere. Were they near the ocean? Her clothes were out there, lying on the bed, and she didn't *feel* alone.

'Hello? Who's there?'

A sound like breathing.

She swallowed, got a better grip on her towel, and twisted her head around the door to see into the room. It was no good. She couldn't see into the room without putting her undressed self into view. She glanced down and saw that she was covered, but

anyone looking would know there was nothing
behind the towel, nothing covering her naked back
and buttocks.

The man who had rented her the room had
seemed polite and courteous. She was a good judge
of character and she was certain she was not wrong
about him. It could be Joe. She swallowed and felt
the conviction that it *was* Joe. He had come back,
whether to apologise or to get into another argument
she had no idea, but whichever it was——

Whatever his reason for being here, she was going
to send him right back out of the door! He wanted
to sleep in the car and he was darned well going to
sleep in the bloody car or pay for his own room.

Did he have money for a room? She shoved that
thought away. He was a capable man. If he was short
of money he could go into business fixing radiators
or something. It wasn't her problem. She took a deep
breath, got rid of any friendly thoughts towards Joe
the drifter, and strode out into the room.

'Look, this is my room and——'

He was lying on the bed, her bed, the one without
the lumps. His eyes were closed and his arms were
crossed over his naked chest. He had taken off his
shirt, his shoes and socks. She watched as he drew
in a deep breath. She saw the muscles of his chest
expand and flex as his lungs filled. He turned,
thrusting out one leg in an unconscious move for
comfort. The denim of his jeans pulled tight,
exposing his masculine shape.

Dinah shuddered, found her tongue licking her
lips. Here she was, twenty-six years old, not even
interested in the man, and the sight of his half-naked
body was sending her heart wild, her breath choking

in her chest. She bit her lip and tiptoed into the room, grabbed her clothes out of the suitcase and ducked back into the bathroom.

At least he'd left his jeans on.

CHAPTER FOUR

DINAH woke to the sound of water.

Thin blankets over her, twisted because the night had been too hot. The smell of something spicy coming through an open window. The sound of water and a man humming tunelessly.

The hotel room. A village she didn't even know the name of, somewhere in Baja California. Mexico. She breathed deeply, taking in the smell of someone's breakfast from outside. It smelled good. Exotic and strange, but good. The water stopped and she opened her eyes then. There was no one on that other bed, so it was Joe in the shower, Joe who couldn't hold a tune, but seemed to enjoy trying as he showered.

Her suitcase was where she had left it on the floor. She'd been angry last night: partly because he'd had the nerve to come back and fall asleep as if she would welcome him; partly because he'd taken the comfortable bed. Damn it! She was the one who had paid for the hotel room!

She had packed only one sun-dress. It was lying at the bottom of the suitcase, wrinkled and crushed. She pulled off the oversized T-shirt she'd slept in and replaced it with the dress. It wasn't the kind of dress you could wear a bra with, but it was loose enough that maybe the soft thrust of her breasts wouldn't be too obvious. The important thing was to stay cool. No more blue jeans. They were killers in the heat.

She had her suitcase done up and was carrying it to the door when he came out. He still didn't have a shirt on. She kept her eyes away from the damp curl of the hair on his chest, and found herself looking down at the floor. Damn! What was it about the man? There was even something erotic about his bare feet spread out on the hard floor, the line of fair hair on their tops.

He said, 'Morning,' hardly looking at her. He was no more talkative than he'd been the day before. He scratched the damp hair on his chest absently, and she could smell the clean, soapy freshness of him, mixed with something musky and intimate, his personal scent.

She said, 'Morning,' trying to be as curt as Joe, but somehow it didn't work and she was grinning at him. 'I thought you were going to sleep in the car.'

'Yeah, me too. It was the bed. It looked pretty tempting.' He came across the room and she had to force herself not to back up. What was it about this man that was so incredibly masculine? He was good-looking, but not unusually so; muscular, but probably not more so than any husky lumberjack.

She picked up her suitcase, and concentrated on looking around the room for anything she had missed. 'I locked the door,' she said deliberately. 'Last night. I locked the door before I took my shower.'

'It wasn't much of a lock.'

She glanced at it and supposed that, if you knew about locks, you could open it. Lord knew what kind of skills the man had picked up. It didn't seem worth making an issue of. It wasn't as if he'd done her any harm, just used the bed she would have liked to have, although she had an uneasy fantasy that he might have stood at the bathroom door, looking at her naked silhouette through the shower curtain.

'Well, I'm going.' Her words seemed ridiculously unnecessary with the suitcase in her hand. 'I'll put the suitcase in the car and then try to find breakfast. I can smell something pretty good out there.'

It was a taco stand across the street from the hotel. She crossed and stood there eating spicy tacos for breakfast. They tasted better than anything she could remember eating in years. She had two and handed over some of the big Mexican coins in return. Joe joined her and devoured three of the steaming tacos. The Mexican man standing beside Dinah asked Joe a question and she listened as they talked, catching something about La Paz and nothing else. Then the Mexican left, smiling widely at Dinah, and she was left alone with Joe.

'At least you put your shirt on,' she murmured. The shirt was another T-shirt, somewhat less tattered than yesterday's. It looked good on him, the cotton knit pulling tight across his muscular chest. She tried to tell herself she didn't care what he looked like. He'd put on sandals, too, and she wondered again how his bare feet could seem sensual. They were a little bony. They certainly had no objective claim to beauty.

He said, 'It's not acceptable for a man to go around bare-chested in Mexico, unless he's at the beach.'

She was surprised. 'I didn't think you'd care what people thought.'

He shrugged, wiping his mouth with the back of his hand. 'I don't go looking to offend people. You ready to go?'

She was driving this time. She had decided that last night while she was trying to sleep, listening to his breathing in the bed beside her. She went to the car and got in the driver's seat while he put his duffel bag in the boot. While she waited for him she got Cathy's letter out of her bag and looked at it again.

Leo
    Pete left me. I'm in trouble, and I don't know what to do about the baby when it comes. Please, Leo, could you send me the money to come home? Send it to Poste Restante here in La Paz. I'll do whatever you want if you get me out of this mess. I'll even go back to school.
    Cathy

Joe settled in the passenger seat. Still looking at the letter, Dinah asked, 'How many people are there in La Paz?'

'Hundred and eighty thousand.'

She sighed. Too many. 'Do you—Joe, do you have any idea how I could go about looking for a Canadian girl there? I—I don't know her last name, or her address. I just know she—she was in La Paz.'

'How do you know that?'

She handed him the letter. He frowned as he read it and she saw another Joe, a man who could be troubled by the plight of a young girl alone in a strange country. She hadn't expected that. He said slowly, 'February. She was in La Paz in February.' His frown encompassed her. If he was going to tell her she was a fool, that she should go home, this would be the moment for the words. Her fingers clenched until she could feel the nails digging painfully into her palms. 'That's the last you know? La Paz in February? She could be anywhere by now.'

She swallowed. 'I know. I—there was nothing else I could do except come and try to find her.' He was staring at her and she said defensively, 'She wrote for help.'

He lifted the thin piece of paper. 'She wrote to a guy named Leo.' He didn't say it as if he were arguing. 'It's the same thing.' She closed her eyes and saw Leo's face as he'd opened the car door for her that night. She had telephoned, frightened and alone, and he had come. 'Leo would help her if he could, so I've got to.'

The paper fluttered down. His face had closed down and that other Joe was gone. 'Who is Leo? Why should you——? No, don't answer that!' His voice was sharp, like a weapon. 'How the hell did I get into this, anyway?' He closed his eyes and she could feel the anger in him, could not understand it, but knew it was real as he gritted out, 'How did I luck out and end up taking you on in the middle of the Baja?'

She blinked, unprepared for his attack or for the crazy way it cut her somewhere deep inside. He glared at her. 'What are you, Dinah? Are you going to be the albatross around my neck?'

'Get out!' She should have known that he would not help. Another test, but this time she felt a sick pain. She hadn't wanted Joe to fail, but should have known he would. Warren she hadn't cared about, but somehow Joe she had believed in, despite the drifter's eyes.

She took the letter from his fingers, shoved it into

her bag. Then she got her fingers around the steering-wheel, gripped hard and stared ahead. 'Get out of here!' She swallowed. 'I didn't ask for you. I certainly don't want you to be a traitor to your wonderful life of drifting through the world like some ghost that doesn't belong.'

She heard his breath drawn in, as if she had scored a painful hit. She held tighter on to the steering-wheel. 'Just go away, would you, and find someone else to drive you down this God-awful desert! Use that key you've still got in your pocket, get your damned bag out of my boot and take off!'

She turned and faced him, their eyes meeting for the first time since she had handed him Cathy's letter. His eyes were hard and the blue was like ice. For one incredible instant she thought he was going to kiss her, and wondered what kind of kiss it could be with the terrible cold in his eyes. She had the crazy conviction that their words had nothing to do with the argument, that they were fighting over something much deeper than Cathy and whether a drifter would help.

When he got out, she forced herself not to look back, not even in the mirror. His face had showed nothing and she made sure that her expression was a mirror of his. She felt the car shift when he slammed the boot down, then the keys fell into her lap. She could feel him standing there outside her door.

'Don't use the air-conditioning.' His voice was toneless. 'Shift into second gear when you're going up the hills. If it starts pinging, then turn on the heater.'

She swallowed. She was behaving like an idiot and she knew it. He was walking away, the duffel bag over his shoulder. On the other side of the street

he turned and started walking towards the highway.
A truck came up behind him and he shifted the bag
and stuck his thumb out. The truck stopped.

She wasn't even sure what had happened. She'd
picked up a hitch-hiker, and now she'd kicked him
out and she felt a grey barrenness like the time when
she'd woken up in hospital and they'd told her that
her parents were gone. Why? Joe was no one, just a
man who was admittedly attractive, who somehow
stirred her dormant sensuality—

Dormant? She grimaced, admitting that he'd
stirred desires she really hadn't known she
possessed. She'd decided years ago that sex was very
overrated, that she for one could do without it. Leo
said she had a hang-up about men, but she didn't.
She'd worked all that out in her mind and she was
probably as normal as the next woman, or at least
as normal as any other woman with a low sex drive.
From everything she had read, that didn't
necessarily put her in the minority.

So maybe she'd miscalculated. Maybe there was
something there, after all. She'd been staring at a
man's hairy feet and getting turned on, for goodness'
sake! Maybe she was a late bloomer, although surely
twenty-six was a bit much for delayed blooming?
Whatever it was, her reaction to Joe had made her
pretty irrational. He'd been irrational too, as if her
search for Cathy threatened his equilibrium.
'Albatross around his neck'! She hadn't asked for
anything, just information!

She made a production of putting her spare key
back into the magnetic holder, fixing the holder back
under the bumper. Three brown-skinned boys
watched the whole process curiously. She hoped she

wasn't teaching them where to look for keys to strangers' cars. It didn't really matter that Joe had gone. Really, she was relieved that he'd left. Maybe she had been thinking about a relationship, but not with him. She wouldn't be crazy enough to get involved with a man like that, would she? No roots, no job. A drifter, the kind of man who could make a girl forget she had her own home, her own place in the world.

She got into the car and made sure all the windows were down. She had her hand on the key when she thought to wonder how much water was in the radiator. The rad was cold now, and she wasn't going to get into the position of having to open it hot if she could help it. Joe's manoeuvre with the newspaper yesterday had looked dangerous enough that she did not want to try it.

It took a half-gallon before it was full. Two litres, she corrected, thinking of Joe's criticism about her poor conversion to metric. She put the cap back on and felt a little better, more like the Dinah Collins who had started out on this journey. Efficient. Self-confident.

She found a store that was open and purchased two more gallons of distilled water. Two gallons . . . eight litres—whatever the two containers were, they were water and she had a good reserve if she had to stop. She wasn't going to do Joe's stunt with the newspaper. If she had to stop again, she'd sit there and drink pop and wait for things to cool off enough to touch. That reminded her to buy some Coke, too, although she knew it wouldn't stay cold in the car. As soon as that sun got up high, it would be a scorcher!

By the time she did start the engine and put the

Olds into gear, she was pretty sure the truck that had given Joe a lift would be long gone. She waved at the three boys and they grinned and said goodbye in English. She still didn't know the name of the village. She didn't see any sign on her way out.

Joe was at the highway, standing at the side of the road with his thumb out. The truck must have dropped him there, must have been travelling north. She pulled on to the highway. His head turned when her wheels crunched, and his thumb dropped the instant he recognised the car. He didn't want a ride from her. She hit the accelerator and got herself past him. He was staring at her all the way, and for miles she could feel his eyes boring into her back.

The car behaved nicely all through the morning. By noon she had decided that everything would be OK if she left the air-conditioning off. She drank three bottles of soft drink, each one warmer than the last. She didn't want to stop, didn't want Joe to pass and see her. She wanted to do better without him than with him, to prove she didn't need him.

Of course she didn't need him!

She stopped briefly in a village to buy more supplies. She would eat lunch on the road, not stopping. For some reason most of these villages weren't even on her map of the Baja, and she never seemed to see any sign announcing their names. This one was a collection of a hundred or so houses and a small grocery store. She went in and found that all the cheeses were white and strange to her. She used sign-language to persuade the clerk to give her a taste of one cheese. It was very good and she bought a small piece. Tortillas, too, and cold soft drinks. In this heat she found herself constantly thirsty. By the time she left the store, she had her arms full.

Her best purchase was a small polystyrene cooler and some ice. Now her soft drinks would stay cool! She drove through the village and back to the highway, waving to a uniformed policeman directing traffic at the one busy intersection and getting a wide grin in return.

It was the hottest part of the day, early afternoon. She began climbing another mountain, perhaps the highest of them all. Somewhere on the winding slope she realised she could smell steam inside the car. She turned the heater on, taking turns with her feet and trying not to get burned by the hot air blasting her accelerator foot.

The Olds crawled slowly up to the peak of the world and she had an incredible view of the Gulf of California. But there was more. She went up and up, one eye on the place where the temperature light would come on, hoping she would make it to a turn-off and not have to repeat yesterday's fiasco. As usual, there were no shoulders on the road, nowhere to stop. Finally, she reached a plateau and found a side-road to turn off on. The temperature light went on just as she left the highway. So she would stop here a while. If Joe passed, he might not notice her. She was far enough off the road that he and his ride might just drive on by and never know.

She raised the bonnet. Of course, there was no shade, only cacti, but eventually things would cool off. She stared at the radiator for a while, waiting for it to cool, but that was futile. She might as well relax, resign herself to an hour or two of waiting.

She walked through the cacti, away from the road.

There were quite a few different green things growing here, but they were all unfamiliar to her. Some of the cacti rose to the height of apple trees. A good lunch stop.

She got her picnicking blanket from the boot and sat on the ground on the shady side of the car, breaking out the tortillas and cheese. They tasted wonderful, although she should have thought to get something in the way of fruits or vegetables to go with her lunch. She'd been bewildered by the assortment of fruits in the little store. The bananas she had recognised, but the others were exotic and mostly far too large for one person. The bananas, unfortunately, had been black and distasteful. She had been tempted to buy a pineapple, but she had no knife to cut it with. The cooler and ice-cubes had definitely been her best buy! The Coke was cool and delicious.

She closed her eyes and shifted her skirt up to expose her legs to the slight breeze, swallowing and delighting in the sensuous ecstasy of cheese and Mexican tortillas, the hot sun beating on her skin. When she felt dry, she lifted the Coke without opening her eyes and swallowed a long, cool drink of liquid.

'Enjoying yourself?'

She jerked, her eyes flying open. He was blocking out the sky, standing in front of her, his thumbs hooked in his belt. His voice sounded friendly, easy, not angry at all.

'Hi, Joe.' She found herself smiling at him and wondered if she hadn't been expecting him, waiting for him. She asked, 'You got a ride?' He hunched down beside her and she remembered her skirt and pulled it over her legs.

He was smiling. 'More comfortable than the jeans? Cooler, I'd bet.'

'Much.' She'd missed him. Of course he was a drifter, but he had been good company and she would like him back, sharing the Baja with her. 'You need a ride?' His eyes sheared off to the open bonnet and she said, 'In a while. When things cool off. I don't think I'm going to get to La Paz today. Maybe tomorrow.'

If he said yes, there would be another hotel tonight. Her insides shuddered at the thought. She was playing with fire and she wasn't sure if she wanted to step back. Here today and gone tomorrow. That was the kind of man he was. Their eyes held and she thought wildly that perhaps that was best. This crazy wildness would be too much to let into her life for anything more than a . . . a night.

'Do you want a tortilla? And a Coke?' Oh, lord! Her voice sounded as if she were inviting him into her bed . . . into *herself*.

'Yes to the Coke. No food, though. I had lunch in Santa Rosalia.' He opened her little cooler and helped himself to a tin of the cool soft drink. 'This cooler was a good idea,' he said when he'd downed half the tin of liquid in one long swallow.

'Wonderful idea.' She grinned. 'I'm starting to talk like you, leaving off the little words. I bought it in a little town back there somewhere. Maybe it was Santa Rosalia. I didn't see a sign. How did you get here?'

He drained the tin, then reached for one of the tortillas he had refused a minute ago. She held out the cheese and he brought out a pocket-knife and sliced himself a piece. '*Rancherito*,' he said, swallowing his first bite. 'That's local cheese. My favourite.'

She felt a crazy glow of pleasure. 'I like it too.' Her conversation was the height of trivia, but inside she felt good. She hugged to herself the knowledge that he must have told his ride to stop and let him out here. He had seen her car and had stopped. 'I'm glad you're here.'

He didn't say anything, but his eyes found the line of her dress above her breasts. She hoped he couldn't see her heart slamming into her ribcage. He looked away, studied a big cactus. 'How's the car behaving?'

'Hot.' That wasn't a bad description for how her body was behaving, what with the sun overhead and the man crouched down on his heels in front of her. 'It'll cool off.' The car would, but would she? 'I don't think it's as bad this time. I had the heater on and I was pulling off the highway when the light came on. So I don't need help.' He was here. She supposed he had stopped because she might be stranded, not because she made his heart race. She pushed down the thoughts that shouldn't be racing wildly around, the fantasy of passionate lovemaking here under the sun.

She said nervously, 'If you want to do your stunt with the newspaper and the rad cap, I could get on my way a bit quicker. And I'd like company on the drive. It's a long way.'

'OK.' He stood up and went to look under the bonnet. 'Let's leave it a bit longer to cool off. There's a lot more mountain up ahead of us. We'll explore while we wait.'

He made her lock her bag in the boot with his before they went walking. They took two more soft drinks out of the cooler and shut up the car, leaving the bonnet up and the windows open an inch on the top. Then they went off through the cacti, sipping their drinks. Joe led her, following the track a goat might have made. He made sure she kept clear of the little scrub bushes.

'I don't know if there are rattlesnakes around here or not,' he told her, 'but the country's got that look, so we'll just walk in the open and avoid trouble.'

She smiled at his back, echoing his words. 'Walk in the open and avoid trouble. Is that your motto, Joe?' How old was he? Thirty-five?

'Could be.' He had reached the top of a small rise and he turned back to watch her climb up the slope. 'What's your motto?'

'I'm not sure.' She reached his side and turned to look back. 'Oh, it's beautiful!' They were high enough to look down over rolling mountain peaks, on and on to the straight blue line that was the ocean. 'It's water, isn't it?'

He nodded. 'The Sea of Cortez. More recently called the Gulf of California. It's good cruising ground.'

'Is that where you take your boat?' From what she could see, it was a pretty big body of water. 'My geography's not exactly my strong point, but isn't it pretty wide?'

'Anywhere from one to three hundred miles, and six hundred miles long. But the water's warm and the conditions are pretty benign most of the time. I've been cruising here for a couple of years now. Good fishing. Friendly people. Easy living.'

She frowned, staring at the blue. 'Is that enough? It sounds like a holiday from life.'

'I'll be moving on soon, heading for the South Pacific.' That wasn't an answer, and the South

Pacific was a pretty vague destination.

'Do you ever think about going back?' She turned to see his face, and it was a little too carefully blank. She was treading on thin ice here, asking forbidden questions.

His eyes focused on her, and this time there didn't seem to be any anger in them. He said simply, 'What makes you think there's a place to go back to?'

She thought of herself all those years ago, running up to the road from that beach, crying and knowing there was nowhere to go back to, no one who wanted her. 'There's always a place you can start,' she said quietly, thinking of Leo, swallowing because Leo's going was an empty place in her life that could not easily be filled.

She turned away from the memories and focused on Joe's face. There was something there, a window on a world he had walked away from. 'I don't know what you're running from,' she said softly. 'But I don't think you're the kind of man who can be satisfied with a life that doesn't contribute anything. Don't you think it's time you came back from your holiday?' She smiled, trying to take the sting out of her words. 'I've been working for my boss for two years. I get three weeks' holiday every year. How long have you been on holiday?'

'Three years.' Joe made his voice expressionless, revealing nothing of the way her words brought back all the memories. Three years spent walking away from nothing.

The first year had been like a race. He had sailed off and kept moving, hardly even talking to the people on the other boats he'd met. He'd circumnavigated the world in just over a year, ended up in Mexico exhausted and a couple of thousand miles from the place that had been home. Their loss had still been an ache, but dulling.

Now she was standing there, watching him, and he heard his voice saying, 'You have a very unsettling effect on me.' Her eyes widened and he said carefully, 'I don't want to be unsettled.'

'No,' she agreed. 'I knew that.' But she blinked her grey-blue eyes and he could feel his heart trying to crash its way out of his ribcage. He wanted to reach out, touch her, hold her tight against him until her softness swelled against him. He would kiss her, brush her lips and invade the sweet darkness of her mouth. Then . . .

She said, 'I don't want to be unsettled either.' Something flashed in her eyes and she added, 'Not exactly.'

They were alone, in the middle of the mountain desert. If he touched her and she turned to fire, he would undo those flimsy little ties at her shoulders and the dress would fall. She had hardly anything on under it, he knew that. His eyes had been fighting to stay away from the soft hints of her body ever since early this morning when he'd first seen her. Her white creamy flesh would be exposed, waiting for him. He swallowed the powerful image and managed to ask, 'What does that mean? Not exactly?'

Her tongue slipped out to wet her lips. His fingers reached out towards her, but he got them back. Was he crazy? He couldn't take her here in the middle of the desert! He pulled facts in to cool his blood. Scorpions. Tarantulas. That would be a hell of a come-down, interrupting a hot desert interlude with a tarantula bite!

'It means . . .' She swallowed and he saw that she was going to be honest. He wished she would keep herself hidden more. It would make it easier to do whatever they were going to do together, then walk away. If it was going to happen, it should be cooler, with more distance between them. Otherwise——

'That when this is over . . .' He saw her throat move again. She wet her lips and her voice turned brisk. 'You unsettle me, too. I——Whatever happens, I want to be able to go back afterwards, to go home to my job and my life, and I don't want to—I don't want to be different, to be hurting or . . . anything.'

He came closer. He could see her chest moving unsteadily. Her breathing was giving her trouble. So was his. 'Dinah,' her name came out as a hoarse whisper. Wasn't that what he wanted too? No more hurting. He felt a painful urge to tell her about Julie and Sherrie and Bruce, about the Joe that had existed before it had all become impossible. He said, 'I don't know who you are,' and he wasn't sure what his words meant. 'Hurting is a pretty personal thing.'

He was going to touch her. He wasn't sure why, whether it was because of the hardness of his body, or the need to avoid opening up with words. She was only inches away, and her lips were waiting for him. He managed to say, 'I'm not going to ask anything of you. Just whatever happens here . . . Nothing more.'

Her lips were soft, trembling. The shy uncertainty of her mouth surprised him and he drew back a little, brushing her lips with his, taking the sweetness carefully, then more as she trembled and her mouth opened to him. He hadn't wanted to desire her so much. It was like a wild thing in him, the need to bury himself in her, to feel her surrounding him, touching his body and his heart and soul.

He kept his hands at his sides, a crazy attempt to keep his sanity. She shifted, her lips coming against his more positively, her tongue touching his. He bent to her then, but forced himself to feel the difference, her tallness and the strength of her body as it waited for his touch. Julie. Julie had been small and fragile.

Soft, unrestrained breasts brushed lightly against his chest, exploding Julie's memory as a harsh need surged through him. He reached for her, drowning in her warm, woman's scent, seeking out the softness that sheathed her firm body.

Dinah felt her knees give way when his hands settled on her waist. Her blood was boiling, just like that radiator! She sagged against him, knowing the instant before his hands touched her that he would take her weight, holding her close, his hands running up along the loose dress, feeling the flesh that covered her ribs, the small, hard muscles of her back, the softness that trembled over the muscles.

His mouth hardened. She felt her heart working to keep up with the rush of blood that sang everywhere in her veins. Then his hands slipped down, cupped her buttocks and held her close, and she thought she was going to die from the shuddering wave of need that possessed her. She slid her arms around his neck and held on while the world rocked.

His mouth drew away from hers unwillingly, lips seeking the curve of her cheek, the sensitive underside of her jaw. Her head lost its equilibrium and fell back along his shoulder, the soft hair rummaging against his chest as if it had come home. Her fingers explored the ridges at the back of his neck, the hard muscle that led to his shoulder.

He bent, holding her close with one hard hand splayed against the small of her back. She found the ridge of his collarbone and traced it to its source as his lips opened on the flesh that swelled softly just above her breast. Sweet . . . shuddering pleasure . . . Lips hot and soft on her. There was a shifting, a touch at her shoulder and the thin tie dropped from the right side. His teeth took the edge of fabric and pulled gently down, his head ducking as he freed her breast.

Her fingers were knotted in his hair, gripping. Her eyes must have been closed because there was only heat on her eyelids, no vision, and she felt the hot sun touching her exposed breast with an erotic caress that made her swell. A groan escaped her lips as his tongue caressed the warm slope leading to her hardening nipple, the hairs of his moustache brushing against her sensitised flesh.

'God, you taste good!' It was a low groan as his lips found their goal, his throat sucked to draw the turgid peak into his mouth.

Ohhhhh . . .

She didn't know if her throat sent the sound. There was a roaring everywhere. It might be the wind that would end the world, or it might be in her, around her . . . them. Her stomach was caving in with the harsh breathing that couldn't keep up with the spinning in her head. Her fingers clutched his hair and the soft lobe of his ear as he tongued the sensitive peak of her swelling woman's arousal.

When he left her breast with a soft, sucking caress she found her eyes open, staring into his, her head pillowed in his arm as if it could not move. His hand touched, cupped the swelling he had kissed so shudderingly, and he saw in her eyes what his touch did. A blue flame answered her need and she thought she would never be able to breathe again. He pulled the cotton of her bodice up, covering her, dragging it across her nipple with a slow caress that made her shudder.

'Joe . . .'

She saw him swallow, could not help seeing the hard evidence of his need as he stepped back from her. His tongue wet his lips and his throat worked again, then he managed a husky voice.

'You're dynamite, lady.' He couldn't breathe either. His fingers fumbled at the ties of her dress, but he failed to get the bow. He clenched his fingers, and said, 'I'm not exactly prepared for this to go any further.'

Not prepared. She remembered telling Sally that she was crazy to walk into a wild relationship with a man without thinking. That these days, if a woman was even going to think about being with a man, she'd better make a trip to the chemist's first.

'I . . .' She wanted him. Out here, under the sun, with the cactus looking on. She wanted him. She closed her eyes, told herself harshly and silently that she wasn't that crazy. 'I'm not prepared either,' she managed finally, her words a triumph of will and sanity over the things his eyes and his touch did to her body.

She saw the air leave his body. He had been holding his breath as if he wanted her perhaps as wildly as she needed him. 'That's that, then,' he said. He cleared his throat. 'Why don't I see about the rad while you . . .' He pushed back his hair, rubbed the back of his index finger along his moustache. Her eyes widened with the remembered touch of his moustache against her breast. His voice was hoarse. 'You'd better do up your dress. If I do it . . . try to do it, we're not going anywhere.'

He watched her fingers fumbling, watched as the tie was knotted over her shoulder. Then he took in a deep breath. 'Goddammit, Dinah. You——' He choked off something that might have been a laugh, but wasn't. 'I haven't felt so——' He broke off and spun around to head for the car.

Neither had she felt so . . . not ever. She retied the shoulder of her dress, making a neater job of it this time. So this was what Sally found so exciting. Or had Sally ever felt like this? Had anyone? She swung around, making herself look away from his disappearing back, trying to still her mind and erase a picture of Dinah Collins going into a chemist's and making certain that next time, if there was a next time, she was ready for him.

Would she have the nerve to make a purchase like that? Some of the girls she took camping, like Sally, were sexually active. She didn't try to tell them not to, that would have turned them away from her and probably wouldn't have stopped anything. After all, Dinah's role was as a friend, a big sister to the girls. They went camping, and she tried to be a role model to show them that there were ways a girl could make it on her own, be a woman with pride and self-respect. So she didn't talk about the morals, but made certain they knew the facts about protecting themselves. Lord, Sally would laugh if she knew that Dinah had never walked into a chemist's and bought anything of that nature!

And now, thinking about doing it for the first time in her life, she realised that it was next to impossible. They spoke Spanish in this country, and that particular purchase was not going to be in her phrase-book!

Just as well, she decided, as she made her way back to the car. This was insanity. She mustn't even think of it. She could close her eyes and see his face, his eyes searching hers, and she'd only known him a day. What if she did ... if they did, and she went home and he became the thing she dreamed about, loving and touching and wanting? What if her days turned empty and sterile and she couldn't find any joy in the world again without him?

'I'll drive first,' she told him later, when the rad was filled and the bonnet down. She didn't meet his eyes, just went to the driver's door saying, 'It's flat country here. You can have the next mountain. You're better at mountains than I am.'

He slid into the passenger seat without speaking. She settled herself, then turned on the engine. 'You're probably better at casual affairs, too,' she added tightly. Oh, lord! Why had she said that?

'Probably.' His voice was expressionless. He didn't look at her, just shifted down and leaned his head back. She sneaked a look and his eyes were closed. He felt her eyes on him, must have felt them, because he said, 'Don't worry, *señorita*. Nothing happened. Nothing at all.'

What about the feeling inside her, the turmoil of nervous feelings she had never felt before? It was almost as tremulously frightening as thinking of tonight when dark fell, of the man at her side and, somewhere ahead, a hotel.

CHAPTER FIVE

JOE slept in the passenger seat while Dinah drove. There were mountains. She took them slowly, and turned on the heater for one steep grade. Whenever she looked across at him, she felt an intimacy, a pull from somewhere that was her heart or her stomach. Unsettling.

He stretched and rubbed his eyes as she negotiated a narrow street and parked in what seemed to be the middle of the little village she had found.

He tried to stretch his legs, but there wasn't room. 'Where are we? I—— Oh, it's Loreto. Too bad I slept while we were going along Conception Bay. We could have stopped for a swim. Cooled off.'

She had no bathing suit and she found herself wondering if she would have gone into the water in only her panties. She had nothing else under this dress. She asked, 'Where do you think for dinner?'

She had a restaurant in mind, but Joe overruled her and they ate at a taco stand. Mexican taco stands had to be the least expensive meals in the world, but the eating didn't last long and they were back at the car before she was ready to deal with the issue of where they would stay the night.

He took the keys from her hands and she didn't protest. He had a way of taking over that she should resist, but she did not want to resist, although she wasn't sure where they were going. He managed to get them through the crowded streets, around a Pepsi truck that had stalled in the middle of a major intersection. They passed two *farmacia* signs. She shivered, remembering her fantasy of dashing into a chemist's to make a purchase that would make an affair possible. The car kept going, didn't stop. Just as well, she decided. By tomorrow she would be regretting this wild need.

Then they were on the highway and it was turning into another mountain. She bit her lip and said, 'It'll be dark soon.' She didn't want to mention a hotel. He might think she was suggesting something more than sleep, and she was too confused to know what she wanted.

He was concentrating on the road. He didn't answer.

'Shouldn't we stop somewhere before dark?'

He shifted the car down into second gear, took a *curva peligrosa* slowly and smoothly. 'We'll go on,' he said. 'I'll drive. When you get tired, let me know and I'll stop so you can get into the back to sleep.'

'What about——?' She shifted uncomfortably. What about a hotel? What about touching, sharing, loving? What about a *farmacia*? She swallowed, asked only, 'What about the cows?'

He settled himself in the seat. He was getting comfortable for a long drive. 'There are things more dangerous than cows.' He pushed his fair hair back and his voice wasn't soft at all when he muttered, 'You, *señorita*, are a hell of a lot more dangerous than a cow.'

That was almost the last thing he said to her. They climbed the worst mountain of all just before the sun set, taking a double-hairpin curve that wound almost straight up.

She stared at the horrifying road, and said with forced lightness, 'This must be hell in the winter when it ices up.' They were just north of the tropics and she knew it was a silly joke, but if he had laughed she would have felt better.

At the top he found a wide spot beside the road and stopped. 'Why don't you go into the back and sleep?' His voice had lost the coldness. It was neutral, as if he didn't care. She opened the door and climbed out, then into the back seat.

When he started the car again, he sounded like a tour guide. 'The mountain we just climbed is called Sierra de la Giganta. Now that we're up, we stay up. This flat plane goes on for over a hundred miles.'

It was the last thing he said for a long time. She pretended to sleep. It was dark. He drove faster than he had earlier. The air cooled with the darkness. She lay awake, seeing the back of his head and wondering who he really was, why he had left whatever it was he had left. She felt that he was filled with a frustrated energy, a need to be productive. Would he ever stop and go back?

Why did it matter to her?

She forced her thoughts to Cathy, and finally fell asleep planning her moves once she got to La Paz. There weren't many moves she could plan, because she had no real idea of what the ropes were in this strange exotic country, but she managed a rough outline, a plan of attack.

When she woke, there were lights shining in the car window. She sat up, dizzy and disorientated. Outside, she could see a cement path along the seaside, street lights sending reflections out over the water. They were parked and Joe was just getting out of the car. She found her sandals and stumbled out on to the pavement as he opened the boot.

'Where are we?' Somewhere civilised. Buildings all around, city lights. A taxi-stand just up the way. Shadows of boats out on the water. Sailboats. 'Where is this?'

'La Paz.' He dumped his duffel bag on the pavement. 'Do you want your suitcase?' He jerked his head towards the building behind her. 'That's a reasonable hotel. American style. They speak English—some, anyway.'

'I guess so.' Her suitcase landed on the pavement, then he slammed the boot down and handed the keys to her. His voice was wry, self-mocking. 'Your suitcase. Your keys. A hotel. Anything else you need?'

'My bag.' She felt thick, stupid. 'Do you think they'll have rooms?' He was going to walk away. She could feel it and did not know how to stop it.

'Bound to. It's the off season.' He leaned into the car and handed out her bag, then he went around and locked all the doors before he returned to the pavement and shouldered his duffel bag. 'That's it,' he said finally, his voice businesslike. 'You're delivered.' He frowned, and added brusquely, 'Thanks for the ride.'

She picked up her suitcase. What did you say to a man who had kissed you and turned your world upside down? 'Where are you going?'

He jerked his head towards the boats. 'My boat, if it hasn't sunk while I was gone. Goodbye, *señorita*.' Then he walked away and she realised that she hadn't really believed he was going until she saw him crossing the street, walking along that sea-wall with his duffel bag slung over his shoulder and his body swinging in a seaman's walk in the tight jeans.

She didn't sleep well. For the first time in days she was in a comfortable bed, accommodated in what Joe had termed an American-style hotel. The hotel room they had shared the night before had been much simpler and about a quarter of the cost of this one. She resented slightly the fact that Joe should assume she wanted the more elaborate accommodations, but decided in the end that perhaps he was simply being practical. After all, the people at the desk had spoken quite good English, and she was hardly equipped to communicate in Spanish.

But she had managed, hadn't she? Back there in that village without a name. Some time before dawn she fell asleep thinking of that, dreaming of a man with hard muscles under a tattered T-shirt, gold flecks in icy blue eyes that could turn hot when he touched her.

When dawn came she found that she had succeeded in making a thorough mess of the bedding without getting much rest. She dressed and went out, and told herself all through breakfast that she had to concentrate on Cathy, forget Joe. She must start her search.

She called Sharon first. The telephone connection was bad, a ringing sound hovering around Sharon's voice.

'It's Dinah. I'm calling from Mexico.'

Sharon squeaked, 'You mean you're down there searching for Leo's unknown Cathy?'

'That's right. Sharon, do you have any idea—I just wondered if you might have been back into Leo's files, if——?'

'Look, Dinah, this isn't exactly according to regulations, but—I've been working at it. Actually, worrying at it. I—Dinah, I think from the description you gave that it's got to be Cathy Stinardson. She's——'

Sharon broke off and Dinah heard papers rustling. 'She's seventeen, five feet four, redhead. She ran away from her foster home a little over a year ago and we haven't heard a word from her. She—just a sec while I—there it is. Last September Leo made a note on her file that she was living with a fellow named Peter, that they were hitting the road, going travelling. There——No, I've got nothing on Peter. Dinah, I checked with my brother. He's on the police force and—anyway, he ran it through the computer, but there's nothing. Apparently there's no real way to check if she left the country. She doesn't have a passport. I managed to check that, but it doesn't tell you much. A Canadian can go to Mexico on just a birth certificate, you know.'

'Yeah.' Dinah gripped the receiver, bit her lip. 'OK, thanks, Sharon. I'll—at least I know her last name now.'

'Call me. Let me know if you find her.' Sharon's voice was sympathetic. 'We should be able to do something if you find her. She was a ward of the court and . . . if she'll let us.'

It was already hot when she went outside. At the tourism office an English-speaking Mexican man obviously wanted to help, but had little to suggest. *Migración*, perhaps. Or the *policía*.

At the immigration office she was assured that no foreigner under the age of eighteen could get into

the country without being accompanied by both
parents, or possessing a notarised letter of
permission from the parents. Dinah knew Cathy
could not have had a letter, and that she had
somehow got into the country. In any case, the
immigration authorities could not help, had no
record of the girl.

At the police station she went through several
smiling officers before one spoke enough English to
tell her that they had no record of the Canadian girl.
He assured her, though, that a lack of records at
migración did not mean Cathy was not in La Paz.
She could have had her tourist card validated at a
border crossing and there would be no record in La
Paz in that case.

No one knew anything about a Canadian girl who
had been in La Paz in February. Not the police. Not
tourism. Not the immigration authorities. They were
all too polite to say what they thought of Dinah's
sanity, but as the day went on she realised herself
how futile it was. Warren, damn him, had been right.
What could she do?

Doctors? But everywhere she walked she saw
doctors' offices. There were so many, and would a
doctor tell her if he were treating Cathy?

The stores were open in the early evening and she
bought two loose cotton dresses in a little shop on
the waterfront. They were cooler than her jeans, but
more modest than the sun-dress she had worn on
the last day coming down the Baja. She wasn't about
to wear the sun-dress in town. As Joe had intimated,
the Mexican men were very taken with her
blondeness. She attracted a lot of smiles and
whistles, but found that, although it was sometimes

embarrassing, it wasn't offensive. The admiration seemed to be combined with a courtly air of reverence for her femininity. The other side of machismo, Joe had called it when she'd mentioned it once.

The next day she simply walked, and looked. Along the waterfront, along the streets with their little, crowded shops. Walking. Looking. Hoping to see Cathy. Too hot! Too many memories of Joe, little nudges, hurting with a ridiculous intensity.

She had known the man for only two days. She kept telling herself that, reminding herself that he was almost a stranger. It didn't work.

After the beaches, she walked through the shops, looking for a cute, pregnant, redheaded teenager. In the afternoon most of the stores closed and she found herself out in the street in the hot sun. Siesta time. If she had any sense she'd follow the Mexicans' example.

She went back to her hotel room, showered and lay down on her bed. She tried to think of someone else to ask, somewhere else to look. The post office?

The next morning she spent a frustrating hour talking to first one post-office official and then another until someone produced a man who spoke English. He only confirmed what she feared. Lots of people got mail addressed to Poste Restante. The post office did not keep track of them.

Finally, she went to the hotel desk and asked, 'How would I find someone on a boat?' The clerk shrugged his bewilderment. There were many boats out in the harbour. He wasn't certain he had understood her properly.

* * *

Would Joe be as hard to find as Cathy?

She felt an aching desire to hear an English-speaking voice. Joe's voice. She was wandering aimlessly when she saw a middle-aged woman driving a rubber dinghy up on to the beach. She looked American or Canadian, not Mexican. Middle-aged and approachable.

'Excuse me, could you tell me how I'd go about finding someone on a boat out there?'

The woman straightened from fixing the dinghy rope around a rock. Her hair was reddish, going grey, her face open and friendly. 'What's the name of the boat?'

'I don't know.' Dinah swallowed. She had an awful urge to cry. 'The man's name is Joe.'

'A friend?' Her brown eyes were mildly curious. 'There must be five or ten Joes out there.'

'I don't know his last name.' Why didn't she? Why hadn't she asked?

The woman shrugged. 'Wouldn't help anyway. The yachties go by boat names. Hardly any of us bother with last names for the people. We're kind of an odd outfit, I guess. You're not a yachtie, are you?'

'No. I'm a Canadian, but that's not equivalent, is it?' They laughed together and Dinah added, 'My name's Dinah.'

'I'm Winnie. Is your Joe a Canadian? A Canadian Joe.' Winnie frowned, and muttered, 'I wonder if the fellow on *Free Moments* isn't Canadian? Joe or John or—he was up in the States, but I think he's just—' She broke off, opened her mouth wide and shouted, 'Hey, Russ! Hey!'

A man part way up the beach stopped and looked back. Winnie called, 'Hey, who's the guy on *Free*

Moments?'

Russ walked two steps towards them, stopped and pushed his hands into his pockets. 'Joe. It's Joe. He helped me fix that coupling when it went.' He added something else that Dinah didn't catch and turned to walk away.

Joe. The man who walked away when things got complicated. But he'd helped Russ with his coupling. He'd seen Dinah to La Paz with her overheating Oldsmobile. His eyes were icy, often cold, but there was a lot more underneath.

Winnie was saying, 'He's anchored down by the Gran Baja Hotel. You can get a *ponga* to take you.'

A *ponga* was a open boat with an outboard motor on it. The one Dinah hired was piloted by a young Mexican who showed her to her seat with a flourish and an admiring smile. He didn't speak English, but he was accustomed to looking for boats in the harbour. She said 'Near the Gran Baja Hotel,' and he set out as if he knew what he was doing. He stood up with one hand stretched down to grip the throttle of the outboard, his eyes narrowed, peering forward over the big bow. They meandered through the yachts in a zig-zag pattern, moving fast. When the *ponga* headed for the back of a boat with an American flag, she said, 'It's a Canadian boat.'

He grinned and said, '*Canadiense*,' and she agreed with a smile. After that they made quicker progress through the boats, stopping only to look for the names on boats that had Canadian flags, or no flags at all.

After a while, Dinah forgot her tension and became involved in studying the boats. How many were there? A hundred? Two hundred? Maybe she would come down to the shore with her sketching block later, try to catch the feeling of these boats that came from everywhere in the world. Romance, adventure. She wondered if she had been right in thinking Joe was running from something. This was a world of its own. She was a girl who needed a fixed address, but she had no right to put her standards on to anyone else.

'*Alli*!' The driver pulled back on the throttle and Dinah grabbed the edge of the boat to keep from falling over on the seat. The driver was still standing, his equilibrium amazingly undisturbed as the *ponga* surged on its own wake, coming to rest beside a sailboat.

A faded Canadian flag was flying from the back. The name, *Free Moments*, was painted on the bow. There was a woman on board, hanging wet towels on the lifelines with clothes-pegs. The wind was catching each towel as she placed it, streaming it out in a straight line away from the boat. As the *ponga* drew alongside, she stepped over to the edge.

'Is——?' Dinah's voice broke off. Either it was the wrong boat, or she shouldn't be here anyway. 'I'm looking for a Canadian named Joe.'

The woman looking down at her was in shorts and a tank-top, full-figured and gorgeous. If Joe had this at home, why would he kiss her and touch her as if . . .?

The full lips frowned, then grinned. 'Joe? Are you particular, or will any old Joe do?'

Her grin was infectious and Dinah found herself smiling back, saying, 'I guess I'm particular. Is he around? He might be the wrong one. He's probably the wrong one.'

Please let him be the wrong one! She had been fooling herself, saying it was for Cathy that she was here. For Cathy, yes, but for Dinah, too.

'Hey, Joe! Come on out of there! Company!'

A dusty back emerged from what seemed to be a hole in the back deck of the boat, a voice, his voice. 'Yeah?' His body, stretching, pulling the kinks out of a back that had been too cramped. His eyes, expressionless as they found Dinah. 'Come aboard.' He didn't smile, didn't frown. He walked stiffly, loosening up as he came towards the middle of the boat where the *ponga* was bumping on the side of the boat. He was naked except for a brief pair of swimming-trunks.

He greeted the Mexican in Spanish, then said to Dinah in English, 'Come on, *señorita*, before he puts a hole in my hull with that banging.' He held a hand down and she was fumbling, then found a foothold and was up on the deck with him, terribly aware of his nakedness and of the other woman.

Dinah handed some pesos down to the *ponga* driver. He swept off his hat to her, then backed his boat away, whistling and grinning.

Her name was Alice. Joe introduced her, but didn't explain who she was, what she was to him. Maybe it didn't need explaining. Dinah felt herself frozen inside, wondered how she was going to get through this visit.

She pushed her hair back. She had showered and shampooed it only this morning, but it was clinging damply, tendrils lying against her flesh, intensifying the heat. 'It's cooler out here,' she said nervously. 'I—I really——'

'I'll get a *refresco*,' offered Alice, dropping the towels on the top of a shiny winch and disappearing through a hatch into the bottom of the boat. 'Ice?' she called back. 'We've got ice! Of course you want ice, don't you?'

Joe was still brushing the dust off his naked chest. Dinah had the crazy conviction that she could feel his skin, that it was *her* fingers touching, brushing. 'Yes,' she agreed. 'Ice would be lovely.'

She found herself sitting in a deck-chair, saying stiffly, 'I thought I'd come out and thank you for helping me down the Baja.'

His knee brushed hers as he sat down, his bare flesh, her knee exposed by the sweep of her skirt. Then he was sitting in the other deck-chair, too close. 'I've been sanding the lazarette. I want to get it repainted before I leave.'

'What's a lazarette?' Leave? She swallowed and curled her fingers around the arms of the chair. He was leaving. She knew that. He'd told her before. The South Pacific. She got control, made her hands relax and her mind concentrate on Alice. She forced her lips to return his smile.

He was saying, '. . . aft deck, sort of a hatch for storing ropes and such. I've got my stern-rope locker back there.' He shrugged. 'Well, anyway—how's the search going?'

Alice came back up on deck. She had lean, hard, curvy legs. She looked like Raquel Welch. Dinah made herself smile. 'Thanks for the drink.' *Refresco* must be soda pop, because this tasted like straight ginger ale. She said, 'I haven't found her.'

Alice asked, 'Are you looking for someone? Who is she?'

NO COST! NO OBLIGATION TO BUY! NO PURCHASE NECESSARY!

PLAY "LUCKY 7" AND GET AS MANY AS SIX FREE GIFTS...

HOW TO PLAY:

1. With a coin, carefully scratch off the silver box at the right. This makes you eligible to receive one or more free books, and possibly other gifts, depending on what is revealed beneath the scratch-off area.

2. You'll receive brand-new Harlequin Presents® novels. When you return this card, we'll send you the books and gifts you qualify for *absolutely free!*

3. If we don't hear from you, every month we'll send you 6 additional novels to read and enjoy. You can return them and owe nothing but if you decide to keep them, you'll pay only $2.24* per book, a savings of 26¢ each off the cover price. There is *no* extra charge for postage and handling. There are no hidden extras.

4. When you join the Harlequin Reader Service®, you'll get our monthly newsletter, as well as additional free gifts from time to time just for being a subscriber.

5. You must be completely satisfied. You may cancel at any time simply by sending us a note or a shipping statement marked "cancel" or returning any shipment to us at our cost.

This lovely Victorian pewter-finish miniature is perfect for displaying a treasured photograph— and it's yours absolutely free—when you accept our no-risk offer.

PLAY "LUCKY 7"

Just scratch off the silver box with a coin. Then check below to see which gifts you get.

YES! I have scratched off the silver box. Please send me all the gifts for which I qualify. I understand I am under no obligation to purchase any books, as explained on the opposite page.

(U-H-P-12/90) 106 CIH BA6M

NAME

ADDRESS   APT

CITY   STATE   ZIP

7	7	7	WORTH FOUR FREE BOOKS, FREE VICTORIAN PICTURE FRAME AND MYSTERY BONUS
🍒	🍒	🍒	WORTH FOUR FREE BOOKS AND MYSTERY BONUS
🫐	🫐	🫐	WORTH FOUR FREE BOOKS
🔔	🔔	🍒	WORTH TWO FREE BOOKS

DETACH AND MAIL CARD TODAY

'A . . . a friend. She's seventeen.' She described Cathy in detail and Alice just frowned.

'I haven't seen her, or if I have——' Alice shrugged shapely shoulders, then said, 'Joe, why don't I make the trip to the market while you and Dinah talk?'

Dinah looked at the varnished wooden mast, stared at the ropes and fittings that must all have some purpose. Alice went below, returned in a wrap-around skirt and leaped lightly down into a rubber dinghy. When she had gone, Dinah still didn't know what to say. If Joe was *her* man, she wouldn't walk away and leave him with another woman.

Joe didn't seem to feel the need for many words. He leaned back and sipped on the icy drink, said idly, 'Thanks for giving me an excuse for a break,' then said nothing more. The silence wasn't bothering him, and after a few moments she realised that it was a nice silence, comfortable, that the motion of the boat was subtle and soothing. She closed her eyes.

She heard Joe get up, but it seemed too much effort to look. His footsteps were quiet, as if he were in bare feet. She remembered the sight of his bare feet and resisted the temptation to turn and look. Today he was wearing so little that he didn't bear too much looking at.

Music came over the water. Later she realised that the music was here, coming from inside his boat. Her fingers slackened and the glass was gone, a brief brush of Joe's fingers. She smiled. 'I really shouldn't sleep,' she said with a whisper.

'Why not? Relax, the boat's not going anywhere.' Then he had gone, and she heard after a while sounds that might be sanding. When she opened

her eyes everything was blue and quiet, the wind a
soft caress on her face, a big blue canopy overhead
shielding her from the sun.

Why not? She let her eyes close again and the soft
motion of the boat in the water took over, blending
with the music she could not identify.

It was the splash that woke her. She sat up, felt a
sense of peace and well-being mixed with confusion.
The water. A boat. Joe's boat. She relaxed a little and
looked around, brushed at the drops of water that
had splattered her arms.

'Want to come in?' He was a few feet away,
treading water, licking drops of the salty stuff from
his moustache. 'It's nice. The perfect cure for a hot
afternoon.' Tempted, she looked down at her dress,
and he said, 'Don't worry about it. Strip off to your
bra and panties. None of the other boats are close
enough to know the difference.'

He disappeared in a surge of water and bubbles.
She stood up, trying to see where he had gone. She
saw a glimpse of one white foot towards the front of
the boat. The other boats were all around, but when
she focused on them it was hard to see details. She
fingered the thin fabric of her dress and wondered
if she would be insane, then wondered who would
pat her back if she sat up here on deck, hot and
sweaty and repressed.

'To hell with it.' No one heard her. No one saw,
either, as she stripped off the dress. Thankfully the
bra she was wearing was reasonably modest, and
she wasn't wearing skimpy bikini panties. She was
covered, although heaven knew what would happen
when the water hit her. She hesitated another
second, staring at the water where she had last seen

Joe, then she balanced on the rail and dived in.

The water closed over her with a cool, refreshing wetness. She swam underwater for a few strokes, then surfaced and pushed her hair out of the way. Then she dived down again just as Joe came to the surface. When she was breathless from swimming underwater, she floated to the surface and turned on her back to kick her way in a lazy circle around the boat.

She stayed in the water when he got out. She had her doubts about the modesty of her outfit once it was soaking wet. She closed her eyes to put off the moment of finding out, rolled over and struck out slowly in another circle, this time on her stomach. Eventually she tired and came to a rest hanging on the bottom rung of his boarding ladder. She couldn't see any sign of Joe. She climbed up quickly and found a big towel draped over the chair where she had been sitting. That was nice of him, preserving her modesty without saying anything about it. Quickly, she wrapped herself in the towel.

'Thanks!' she called. 'That was delicious!'

'Wasn't it?' He came up from below, head first, then his bare chest with drops of water still drying. His chest hair had dried in a tantalising swirl that led down towards the waist of his trunks. 'Here's a shirt. It's big, should cover everything while you get your underwear dry.'

What about Alice? Was the other woman ever coming back? Wouldn't she think this was odd, Dinah lazing around in Joe's oversized shirt? Dinah swallowed, then let Joe show her how to use the sun shower to rinse the salt off her body. He had rigged up a privacy curtain around the cockpit and she showered with the contents of the plastic bottle, rinsing the salt off and shampooing her hair for the second time that day, using his shampoo . . . or Alice's. Then she dried and put on his shirt, hanging her underwear on the lifeline with clothes-pegs and trying to pretend it wasn't there.

Joe brought her another cold drink, this time iced water with lime squeezed into it. She joined him in the deck-chairs and sipped, asking, 'Are you going to give me a tour of your boat?' She had forgotten her need to make excuses for coming out here. Except for the thought of Alice off shopping somewhere, being here seemed like the most natural thing in the world. And he was dressed now, in shorts and a cotton shirt. That made it a little easier to look at him without her mind going wild.

'Sure.' He took a deep drink. 'In a few minutes.' He looked at her and grinned. 'That shirt looks better on you than it ever did on me.'

'It's big.' And a good thing! She needed covering for her thighs, something to make it possible to pretend she wasn't naked underneath.

'My brother gave it to me. It was kind of a joke.'

She looked down at the shirt. It was brightly patterned, far too big for him. It was the gaudy kind of shirt one associated with Hawaii tourists, but giant-sized. She wondered about the nature of the joke, and decided not to ask. 'Tell me about your brother.' That seemed a safe enough topic.

'Hank.' Joe was very relaxed. 'He's my oldest brother.'

'Oldest? How many do you have?' She decided that she liked his boat. It wasn't plastic-pretty, but it was neat and looked well-equipped. It looked like a boat that had been places and done it well.

'There are five of us, all boys.' She tried to imagine what a family like that would be like, but it was beyond her experience. He said, 'Hank's the first. I came next, about ten months later. Hank's a psychiatrist.'

She stiffened a little. 'Psychiatrists are pretty establishment.'

'We were all establishment.' He grinned, then asked, 'How many shrinks have you known?'

'One or two.' She played with the glass, turning it and somehow managing not to spill any, although she almost dropped the whole glass. Of course, he hadn't meant it to be a personal, probing question. She said, 'I was a messed-up kid. I saw a few of your brother's colleagues.' He was waiting and she shrugged. 'I'm not messed up any more.'

'No, I can see that.' He smiled, and said quietly, 'If you ever feel like talking about it, I'll listen.'

Her lips parted, but if she ever started opening up to him there would be no end to it. 'I don't do that much—talking about it.' She shrugged, and said honestly, 'I really think making a fuss about your rotten beginnings is the coward's way out, an excuse for not succeeding as an adult.'

'Are you a success, Dinah?' He was turning his drink now, passing it from hand to hand absently, his hands resting in the space between his stretched-out legs.

'More or less. I haven't fulfilled all my dreams, but I'm working on them.' The hair on his legs was fair and curling slightly. If he'd put on jeans instead of shorts, then——No, it wouldn't have made any difference. It was the man, his presence, the wild things in her mind. She looked away, found the red and white pattern of the flag to stare at.

'Tell me.'

That was easier. She sipped on the drink, wishing there were more because it had tasted wonderful. 'I always wanted to make pictures, oil paintings, really good ones. Leo encouraged me, and I got a scholarship to art college. After that——' he didn't want her life story, for heaven's sake '—I got a job. Commercial art. I work for a small company that does commercial art and film documentaries. It's small, but good. Jake—my boss—has won several awards for his films. He's an artist too, and I've learned a lot about Haida Indian art from him. My job is more commercial than creative, though. I do the more mundane things, the layouts for advertising circulars and some graphics for the films, billboards sometimes. I enjoy it. I'm good at it.' She shrugged a little uncomfortably, but she didn't believe in false modesty and if Jake said she was good, then she was. 'When I'm not working, I work on trying to become a better painter.'

He was silent, waiting. She lifted the glass again, but there was only a trickle of moisture left. 'Jake introduced me to the manager of one of the biggest galleries in Vancouver a couple of months ago. He looked at a few of my paintings.' She grimaced, and said, 'He was quite scathing about some of them, but others——When I get enough paintings done, ones that are good enough—well, I might have my own show.' She frowned, then corrected, 'Not really my own show. It would be shared, a few artists' works, including mine.'

'Good for you.' He leaned forward, frowning, the blue of his eyes almost black. 'What about Jake?' She frowned and he said, 'Is he your lover?'

She jumped. 'No! Jake's married. Jenny——'

'That doesn't always make a difference.'

She bit her lip. 'It does to me. It does to Jake.' Was Joe married to Alice? She hadn't thought so, but——

'Do you want more to drink?'

'Please.'

When he came back he was relaxed again. He handed her the drink and sat down across from her. Why had he asked her about Jake? Did he care? His voice had been hard, as if the thought of her lover hurt him. She thought of Alice, of Joe's hand on the woman's flesh. She shuddered.

He said, 'I wasn't a messed-up kid at all. I was an A student, a track star, president of my class. It was later that everything fell apart.'

She was afraid to ask because he would stop talking. She remained very still and he relaxed a bit into the chair, staring at his glass. 'We're talking about Hank, my brother. Hank and I were at university together. He was a year ahead, but we both went to medical school. He was always interested in psychiatry, though, had to know what made people tick, seemed to have a real need to try to straighten them out. I——' He shook his shoulders impatiently. 'That's a long way back, over ten years. History.'

She looked around. From medical school to a yacht on the west coast of Mexico. What came in between? Over ten years, he said. She looked at the lines of his face. A woman? Not Alice, she decided, because his eyes had not followed Alice when she'd walked away. There had been a wedding-ring, a woman. Then something had sent him roaming the world in this boat. He hadn't lost the energy, the drive that had taken him through a demanding university course of studies, but now it was dedicated to this boat.

The boat was well kept. She could see the woodwork shining with varnish, the metal gleaming in the sun. It would take a lot of work to keep it that way. He wasn't a lazy drifter, but he was still a drifter.

'Joe, do you ever think about going back?'

'No.' He shook the mood, smiled faintly. 'You look after your Cathy. I'll look after Joe.'

It wasn't her business. His voice made it plain that she had no right telling him what he should do. For all she knew, maybe her ideas weren't right for him. People had to make their own decisions. Perhaps he and Alice had a whole world planned for themselves, although he should have a woman who touched him more than Alice seemed to.

With a painful revelation, she knew that what she felt for him was much more than liking, far more than lust. It didn't take much intuition to know that Joe would walk out of her life as suddenly as he had appeared, that he would not be looking back when he did it. She knew he was attracted to her, was sure that he liked her too. She had an idea that he had no real commitment to Alice, whoever the gorgeous woman was.

But liking and attraction were shallow emotions compared to the needs surging inside her. If there had been a future in it, she might have been able to fall in love with him. He would be the only man she had ever loved. Until that moment she had not really believed in the overwhelming fantasy emotion of the books. Love. She swallowed, feeling the loss, because there would probably never be another man to stir her this much.

She drew back, her hand leaving his arm, a nervous fear that touching made a pipeline for her thoughts straight into his mind. She stood up, realised that her bare white thighs were on a level with his eyes, and dropped quickly into the deck-chair.

'Joe, I came out here to see you because——'

'I know. You want me to help you find Cathy.' He looked off towards the mountains behind the city. 'How long have you got to look for her?'

'Two weeks. I have to start back in two weeks.' If she waited that long she would be late back to work, but she thought that if she phoned Jake he would understand and let her take an extra week without pay.

He stood up, looking around at his boat. She thought he was counting up the jobs that he had to do. She said dully, 'You're getting ready to go. Is there a lot to do?'

'Quite a bit.' He pushed his hands into his pockets, and smiled absently with his mind only half on his words. 'She's been here in the sea for two years. She's not really shipshape for the open ocean after all that time. I figure on a good week's work before I can get out. I had planned to set sail next week for the South Pacific.'

She said nothing. What could she say? He shrugged. 'All right. I'll help you. Two weeks, but then if we don't find her we've got to give it up.' She winced and he added more gently, 'You can't look forever, *señorita*. And I can't wait forever to head out. July starts the hurricane season in this part of the world.'

CHAPTER SIX

'JOE, do you ever think about going back?'

The trouble was, it was in his mind more than it should be. Dinah, with her soft question. And Hank. He'd called Hank on the telephone from San Diego last week. It was so much less expensive than telephone calls from within Mexico.

Hank's voice had sharpened near the end of the conversation. 'Joe, don't you think it's time you grew up and stopped playing the irresponsible kid?'

Joe had repressed a sharp retort, had said only, 'I'm not ready, Hank. Face it, I might never be ready. There's a lot to see in the world, and I haven't seen it all.'

Hank had asked scathingly, 'Are you seriously saying you might spent the rest of your life circling the globe in a tub?'

Joe had laughed, refused to take his brother seriously. 'Listen, Hank, if I'm super careful of my money and avoid the costly places in the world, I can keep on doing this almost indefinitely. I can't see a lot of reason why I shouldn't. I'm enjoying myself. It's challenging keeping this boat afloat in a storm. Also, I'm meeting a lot of the interesting people in this world. You should think about it yourself. You're closed in up there in Vancouver, talking to messed-up people.'

Hank had laid off then, but the truth was that when Joe thought of going back he was scared. The thought of other people's lives in his hands, the conviction that he didn't want to go back to an active medical practice. This way, it was only his own neck he was responsible for, and that of his crew, whoever they were at the time. Anyone who was experienced in crewing on ocean passages knew the risks, and Joe never took crew that wasn't experienced. Alice, for example. She had crewed on two Atlantic crossings, could turn her hand to anything from the galley to hauling sail.

So he had planned on going on, heading out to sea within a week of getting back to La Paz. He had told Hank that, sent a message to his parents, pushed back the restless stirrings that had been growing for the last several months, that had nothing to do with wanting to change locations or to move on.

Then he had packed his engine parts with the jar of real peanut butter he couldn't get in Mexico, had slung everything on his shoulder and stuck out his thumb in the direction of La Paz—and had run smack into Dinah.

God! He didn't even know what her last name was. He remembered the feel of her soft, warm flesh under his hands, the deep desire that he had thought was gone forever. He could feel it again, just remembering, and he was consumed by the same mixture of reckless need and guilt.

Hank would tell him that it wasn't rational to feel disloyal to Julie after three years. If he was honest with himself, he would admit that the guilt wouldn't have stopped him up there on that mountaintop. Only one thing had stopped them from consummating the desire that had flared so suddenly. If there'd been a chemist's within ten miles, he would have made her his under the hot sun.

He didn't sleep much, thinking of it, and again he dreamed of her. Hank would say it was progress, that it was not Julie in his dream. The fact was, Julie's face was smoothing, losing its detail. Three years, and sometimes it seemed like a lifetime.

Loving was not a risk he was going to let himself take again, but Dinah, the blonde *señorita*, was not about to slip through his life the way everybody else had these last three years. He had walked away from her at the hotel, telling himself it was the last he would see of her, but she would not leave his dreams. If she hadn't turned up at the boat, he would have gone looking for her.

Two weeks. He had promised her two weeks. Some time during those fourteen days he knew they would become lovers. It was there, under the surface, an explosion waiting to happen. It would burn bright and hot and brief, then he would go and his dreams would be empty.

He told Alice that their departure would be delayed by two weeks. She didn't mind. She had wanted a chance to take the ferry to the mainland and spend ten days on the spectacular trip to the Copper Canyon.

Before Alice left, she turned back and looked Joe in the eye. 'I'm just the crew, honey, but don't you think you've taken on the kind of complications that tie a man down?'

'Two weeks,' he repeated, hearing the note of anger in his own voice. 'I'm helping a friend look for a friend.'

Alice said, 'Maybe, but if it turns into

more——Well, let me know so I can look for another boat, will you? It's getting late in the season and I don't want to be stuck here another year.'

'You won't be,' he promised. 'We're going.'

Joe had ideas she had never thought of. He knew the city, knew the patterns of the English-speaking foreigners who visited and lived there. She walked all over La Paz with him for several days, watched and listened while he asked questions.

He checked the yachts in the harbour first. The English-speaking yachts had a radio net each morning and he made an announcement on it, but no one had heard of Cathy. No one knew of a red-headed gringo girl.

They checked the low-cost hotels, although Joe agreed it was unlikely that a girl with no source of income would be staying in even the cheapest hotel.

La Paz had bright, modern supermarkets, but Joe took her to the vegetable market where the farmers sold their produce. This was the least expensive place to shop for fresh food and it was here that he started asking questions.

'What's a *hermana*?' she asked after she had listened to him talking to several of the women who sold their wares in the market.

'Sister.' He pushed his hair back. 'I've been saying that we're looking for your sister. It's simpler, easier for them to understand why you're here.' He was wearing a cotton shirt today, one of the loose *guyaberas* that the Mexican men wore. Under it were his worn and patched jeans.

'Joe, she might not be pregnant any more. She might have had the baby. We don't know when it was due.' A dark-skinned man bumped into Dinah and apologised profusely in Spanish.

When he had gone, Joe grinned and said, 'He was enjoying the chance to talk to you. A blonde——'

'Yeah, I know.' She flushed a little. The constant attention of the Mexican men was beginning to wear on her. 'I feel as if I'm on a stage.'

'You are.' Something in his voice made her flush and she looked away, remembering how his lips had taken hers, how she had wanted him. Then, abruptly, the tension was gone and he said, 'I've been asking about a woman who's expecting, or one with a baby. Either way, if there was a gringo girl hanging around over a period of time they would notice.'

Another day he took her to the caravan parks where many American and Canadian people spent their winters. Then to a rambling Spanish-style building with a palm-thatch roof that he called a *palapa*. The building seemed to be filled with young people, all gringos, mostly artists of one sort or another. Joe introduced her to Tim, the bearded leader of the group.

'If you want a place to sleep,' offered Tim, 'just come on by.'

She tensed inside. 'Thanks for the offer, but I'm comfortable where I am.' Joe looked at her oddly. Only that morning she had talked about moving to a cheaper hotel.

They left the *palapa* on foot, heading back towards the waterfront. It had been Joe's idea that they would be better to walk, that they would find more people to ask if they didn't insulate themselves with the car. She thought he was right. People seemed to be more talkative when they were on foot.

'Take it easy,' said Joe. 'You'll be exhausted in ten minutes if you keep walking at this rate.'

She realised then that she was walking fast. It was early afternoon, and in the heat of the day a brisk walk could easily lead to exhaustion. She slowed, adopting Joe's easy pace, but her voice was tense. 'I don't know how any of those people get any work done in that house. It's chaos.'

His eyes were watching her intently. 'I thought artists liked to work in chaos. What did Tim say that got your back up so much?'

'I . . .' She shrugged. 'Nothing, really. It's just not my kind of place. Too disorganised. Maybe someone in that place will produce a masterpiece, but I couldn't work like that.'

He caught her fingers, said softly, 'You're a funny artist, honey. Dreams in your eyes, as an artist should have, but solid conservatism in your heart. If you really want to get that art show for yourself, you're going to have to let some of those inhibitions go.'

'What do you know about it?' Her voice shocked her, harsh and cold. She pulled her hand, but he would not let go. She whispered, 'That's what Jake said. That I was great at the commercial stuff, but if I was going to make it in the galleries I'd have to let down the barriers.'

She pulled again and her hand was free, letting her breathe again. His eyes were intent on her and she wished she knew what he was thinking. 'Joe,' she whispered, 'why do I always feel like telling you things? Why do I tell you things?'

He shook his head. 'I don't know, *señorita*. But I want you to tell me something now.' Behind him a couple of women walked by, one with a full basket

on her head and the other carrying a baby. 'Back
there. When Tim—— Of course, he was hoping you'd
move in and he had more than just a friendly offer
in mind. I knew you'd put him off, but the way you
reacted——' He pushed his hair back, and said
uneasily, 'It's a hell of a thing to have to ask a woman
in this day and age, but are you a virgin?'

She stared at him. He was frowning, as if the
possibility was a problem. She had thought he could
see right through her, but he could not see anything.
'Well?' he asked again. He wasn't going to give up
on this question.

'Why should it be any of your bloody business?'
Her voice was too trembly and she found her hand
touching her throat as if to still the emotion there.
'What's it to you?'

He stared at her, his eyes cataloguing information
from her eyes, her voice, the way she stood. Finally
he said quietly, 'I'm planning to have an affair with
you, Dinah. If you're a virgin, that changes things a
bit.'

'A bit?' She swallowed. She looked away from him
and saw the water turning white with the afternoon
wind. 'You mean, because you want an affair to be
quick and convenient and . . . over when it's over?'
It hurt, saying that.

'Yes,' he agreed.

She said tiredly, 'You're an idiot, Joe.'

'What does that mean?'

She shook her head. 'It doesn't mean anything,
only words. It means I don't want to talk about it. I
want to find Cathy. I don't want an affair, so if you're
planning one you'd better find someone else. I——
Aren't you forgetting Alice?'

'What's Alice got to do with you and me?'

'I don't know. I don't even know who Alice is.' They had a brief battle of eyes. She wasn't sure who won, although it left her breathless. She said, 'I don't even want to know.' It was an out-and-out lie. She added quickly, 'What's the next step? I mean Cathy.'

'Do you?' There was something new in his eyes, a spark that hadn't been there before. He said, 'I wonder if either of us knows what we're doing.' His eyes passed over her head, towards the water. She had the idea that he was looking for his boat, although there was no way he could see it from here. 'All right. Cathy. I guess we'd better go further afield. Tomorrow we'll try the nearby beaches. There are a lot of people out there in campsites, some of them living on the beach for months on end. It's probably the cheapest way to live in Mexico.'

For dinner he took her to the beautiful seaside restaurant called El Moro, proving that he didn't always eat at taco stands. A Mexican waiter made them welcome with a quiet flourish.

They didn't talk about Cathy over dinner, but about the town and its history. Joe said that the English Cromwell had made a base of La Paz, that the Mexicans referred to him as one of the pirates that had used the Baja as a hide-out. The waiter joined in, half in Spanish and half in English, telling her that the Coromel evening winds of La Paz were named for Cromwell, that the Englishman had often had to wait for those southerly winds to sail out of La Paz bay.

On Joe's recommendation Dinah ordered the mixed rice, and found the plain-sounding dish to be composed of generous quantities of shrimp and ham, as well as many other unidentifiable but delicious components. He ordered *cerveza* for himself, and she had some of the Mexican beer too. The waiter, smiling and enthusiastic, made it his business to help Dinah with her Spanish.

When she came out of the restaurant, she was glad that they had not brought the car. She wanted to preserve the quiet magic of the evening, and driving in La Paz was nerve-racking. The Mexican drivers had a disconcerting habit of ignoring stop signs and playing a game of chicken at every intersection.

They walked slowly along the sea-wall. Joe laced his fingers in hers and swung her hand gently as they moved. Once they stopped to watch a *ponga* tearing along the water through the darkness. Joe said, 'In Mexico, the people have time to smile. For all our technological wonders, the so-called advanced countries sometimes forget how to do that.' He started moving again, swinging her arm lightly with his. 'I bet if you say hello to any Mexican using his language, he'll greet you back and smile.' He laughed then, and added, 'Even if you aren't a blonde *señorita*.'

They passed her hotel and she didn't remind him that this was where she should get off. It was pleasant, an easy going kind of paradise just walking along the sea-wall with him, smiling at the people they passed, saying *buenas noches* and hearing the greeting returned. With Joe's fingers linked through hers, she didn't get the same reaction from the Mexican men. She smiled about that a little, but shook her head when Joe asked about the smile. She didn't want to draw attention to his hand-holding. He might let her hand go free and she didn't want that.

She was falling in love with him. There was nothing she could do about it. Oh, she could push him away, never see him again. That would be the sensible thing and she had thought about it, but it did not seem like an option. Not that she was dreaming impossible dreams. He was a drifter and he had no intention of stopping. She knew that. She knew it would end with pain.

So much for dreams, she thought, as she stared down at his fingers on hers. But then, she had never dreamed impossible dreams, not since she was a child, and of course she wasn't starting now.

He led her to the beach, to his rubber dinghy that was beached among so many others. 'I thought we'd go out to the boat for a nightcap,' he said then, and she realised they had been silent for a long time. It hadn't seemed like silence. There was warmth inside her from the touch of his hand and his thoughts.

Joe pulled the dinghy out into the water, letting it ride on a set of wheels that he had fixed to the back of it. While he put the wheels back up, Dinah took her shoes off to board the dinghy, catching her skirt in her hand to keep it from getting wet.

She had abandoned her stockings days ago, going bare-legged like most of the Mexican women. It was simply too hot for stockings. She was wearing a blue cotton dress tied with a black sash. She'd bought both here in La Paz and they were comfortable and pretty, yet cool and informal. She had bought a poncho and Mexican sandals, too. She was wearing the sandals over bare feet, but there hadn't yet been an evening cool enough to wear the poncho.

Joe's eyes were on her legs as she sat in the dinghy.

'You're tanning,' he said, although he surely couldn't tell that in the dark. 'You are still using the sun-screen, aren't you?'

She nodded. He had taken her to a chemist's for the sun-screen the day she'd sunburned her arms. Now the red had faded and she was building a golden tan on the parts of her that saw the sun.

He started the engine and coasted out through the boats. The water was very still now, the evening breeze gone. His boat was dark except for the anchor light that he had once told her was rigged to a photo cell so that it turned on at dark every night even when he wasn't there.

She climbed up on to the deck while he held the dinghy at the side of the boat, aware of the way her skirt swung and wondering how much of her legs showed to a man sitting in a dinghy below. She looked down at him from the deck and he seemed to be looking at the water, studying something.

'What about Alice?' she asked as he joined her on deck. He was tying the dinghy to something and he didn't answer. She said, 'I didn't mean to ask that.'

She turned quickly to cross the deck and he said, 'Don't walk away.'

'Where could I go?' She swallowed, and said, 'Actually, you're the one who walks away. If I ask a question that touches the part of you that you don't want public, you just walk away, don't answer, change the subject.'

'Then we're both guilty, aren't we?' He came up behind her. He took her hand in his, and when she pulled to free her wrist he held it tighter. Inside her, something snapped and she was back on that beach, back ten years.

'Don't do that.' Her breathing went short. She could feel his fingers imprisoning her everywhere, her body compressing with the tension of his trap. She pulled and it seemed that his grip only tightened until she felt the desperation growing, the knowledge that he was stronger, that she could not escape his trap. She jerked in a deep breath and yanked hard on her arm, but it only hurt.

'Let me go.' It was a growl, low and angry. It didn't sound anything like Dinah's voice. She twisted, positioning her knee. Abruptly, she was free, staggering back and jolting to a wary balance against the lifelines of his boat.

There was tension in his body too. He was watching her as if she had grown horns. There was light from the moon. She could see his nostrils flaring with the tautness of his breathing, felt her own face rigid with wariness. She was uncomfortably aware that she had nowhere to go, no escape.

Abruptly, the tension drained out of his body. As his hands relaxed she realised that her own fingers were curled into fists. He said softly, as if talking to a disturbed child, 'Don't you think you're over-reacting?'

She closed her eyes, felt the darkness surge in with her breath. 'Yes,' she agreed. What had happened? He had grasped her wrist, and perhaps it was the darkness and the water that had stirred the memory, but suddenly it had not been Joe there any more. She swallowed, said, 'I was over-reacting, but don't *ever* do that again.'

'Do what?' he asked, as if trying to clarify directions to the petrol station. 'What am I not to do,

Dinah? Not touch you?'

'No.' She'd dreamed of his touch on her flesh, his fingers stroking as he had stroked a kitten in the street yesterday. 'I don't mean that.' Was that an invitation? She didn't know, wasn't sure if she meant it to be. 'Don't touch me like that. Restraining me.' Her fingers went to her wrist. 'I know it's not rational, just don't ever do that again.' She swallowed, and said, 'Don't use your strength against me.'

He was silent for a long time. Finally he said softly, 'Hank would say there has to be a reason for your saying that. Who did that to you, Dinah?'

He was putting things together and they were adding up. She could see it in his eyes. Her odd reaction earlier when he had asked if she was a virgin. He would be adding two and two and getting seven. 'Who hurt you?'

She pushed her hair back, then shook her head impatiently so that the blonde cloud fell back around her face.

She saw his face, although moonlight wasn't enough to read his eyes. She offered uneasily, 'I'll trade. Tell me who Alice is.'

He said quietly, 'That's an uneven trade. Alice isn't important to me, she's just crew.' He shifted, leaned against the lifelines with his hands slipped into his pockets. 'I don't make ocean crossings alone. A lot of people figure the ocean is pretty empty and they go alone, sleep when they get the urge, leave the boat set on wind-vane and hope they don't hit anything. I figure that's something like Russian roulette. If you do it often enough, you'll get caught one time. I always take crew with me.'

'Alice is crew? She looks like Raquel Welch.' She

could feel herself calming down. That night was so far back, it made no sense that the terror could still be alive.

'We're not lovers.' He said it quietly and she believed him. 'We might have been, if we'd felt the inclination.' He touched her hand, then drew his back as if it had been an invasion. 'I don't know about Alice, but I didn't feel the urge.' His voice dropped and he said, 'My wife died three years ago, and I don't know if I'm still mourning her or not, but I haven't wanted another woman very often. I didn't want Alice. I like her. We're friends, and I think she'll be good crew.' He swallowed and said, 'I'll trade you this, *señorita*. You're the first woman I've really wanted since Julie died. You're the first woman I can touch and close my eyes and not see her.'

It was not a declaration of love. She knew that. It was in his voice that the wife who had died would not be replaced by a blonde *señorita*. Yet she could feel his need, and it was more than the physical desire that had flared between them. His heart was frozen. If she helped him thaw it, it would not become her heart. It would never belong to any woman again. She knew all that, because he told her without words.

'I'll get deck-chairs,' he offered, 'and a drink.'

Mexican beer again. She liked the taste, but wondered how she would get back to her hotel if she kept on accepting drinks. She liked the music he had started while he was below.

'You still haven't shown me the inside of your boat.'

'No,' he agreed gently, 'but if we go down there

now I'm not sure how honourable I might be. You're looking very beautiful tonight.'

'What about Alice?' She played with the glass, knowing it was her turn to confide something. They had made a deal, hadn't they? He'd told her something. Her name had been Julie, and he still loved her. It didn't seem to matter where Alice was, but she asked, 'Where's Alice?'

'Gone on a trip to the mainland. Since I've delayed leaving, she's taken the ferry to Topolobampo. She's getting the train there to go into the mountains and see the Copper Canyon.' He touched her hand gently, caught her fingers and stroked them. 'Your turn, *señorita*. I've turned myself into an open book.'

'An open book? That sounds like a wild exaggeration.' She drew her hand away because it was easier if he could not feel any trembling she might do. 'It was a long time ago.'

'You haven't forgotten, though.'

'Why should I tell you?' She took a drink of her beer and thought about asking for another.

'Have you ever told anyone?' She shook her head and he said, 'Then don't you think it's time?'

Was it? 'Leo didn't ask,' she said unsteadily. Leo had not asked any questions. 'He knew there was something, but he didn't ask. And I'm not hung up about it, not really.'

'No?' He settled deeper into the chair and set his drink down on the deck. 'Do I get to know who Leo is, too, or do I only get one question?'

She smiled. Memories of Leo were always pleasant. 'Leo was my social worker, sort of. My parents died when I was twelve and I was made a ward of the court because there weren't any relatives that counted, no one who could take me on.' She grimaced and admitted, 'I was trouble, Joe. I wasn't an easy kid. I went through several foster homes pretty quick and there was no reason why any of them would want me.'

His fingers tightened on hers and he didn't say anything silly, but she could feel that he knew how alone she had been. She said briskly, 'Well, it kind of went on like that for quite a while. Foster homes, group homes in between foster homes. I was in the north, but I ran away several times, and one way and another I moved around the province. When I was fifteen I ran away to Vancouver, hitch-hiked and ended up getting picked up by police and turned over to Children's Aid there.'

She was silent a long time and Joe suggested, 'And you met Leo?'

'Yes,' she agreed. 'He was a weird kind of social worker. They had me in a transition home, were talking about shipping me back to the last foster home. I wasn't saying anything, but the moment they put me on a bus I was going to be off at the next stop and selling what was left of my ticket. You see, I kind of had a complex by then. Too many people had messed around with my life, and I wanted to make my own decisions.'

'That seems pretty natural.' He spread her fingers and she found them closing around his. 'Tell me what happened next.'

'Leo told me that he knew I was thinking of skipping.' She grinned and said, 'Anyone else would have lectured me and I'd have shut them right out. Not Leo. He gave me his phone number, his home number, the unlisted one that social workers never give out. He said if I wanted to come out on top, I'd better think about playing the system to get there. He said I'd never make it panhandling on the beach, my hand out for change from the tourists. Begging.' She laughed harshly and said, 'Some kind of independence, eh? I told him to stuff his number. I'd look after my own future.'

'What did he say?' He brushed back the blonde hair from her face, a fleeting caress.

'Nothing. He just took my bag and opened it up and put the piece of paper in. Then he told me I didn't need a reason to call. I was a miserable little hoodlum, Joe. I didn't even answer him. I just stared at the wall and finally he left. It should have felt like a victory, but it didn't. I guess I realised even then that he was one person who could help me, and I was crazy to let him walk out of the door. I took off that night, slipped out through the kitchen window when the house mother wasn't looking.'

He didn't say anything. She had told him a lot, but he was going to wait for it all. She thought about the woman named Julie and somehow it seemed like an offering, a crazy attempt to comfort him, to share part of what no one had ever heard before.

'I made it for almost a year. You see things on television, and it seems that a teenage girl can't survive on the streets unless she becomes . . . It's not true. It wasn't true for me, anyway. I stayed with a couple on the beach for a while. They were bumming around, living on next to nothing, and they had a baby. I helped with the baby and we shared what we scored. Food line-ups and so forth.'

She shrugged. 'Then there was a commune, kind of like the place we visited today, the artists. Drugs.

I didn't get caught in that trap, but I saw other people who did. I started to get scared. I was getting by, cooking and minding babies for people who were too stoned to do it themselves, but where was it going? Where was I going? That's what turned me off about that place today. It was the same kind of set-up. I could smell it. Maybe I imagined I smelled it.'

'No,' he said. His fingers stroked hers gently. 'You were right. I only took you there because I thought it might be a lead for Cathy.'

'I know.' She closed her eyes. 'I hope Cathy's not in that kind of trap, but I know she might be. She called for help, though. You see, that's the first step. It means she wants out. She wrote to Leo in February. Last year she called him one night. He went out and came back with her. She stayed in the apartment downstairs with me for a week, then her boyfriend came and she left. Leo was worried about her.'

Joe's fingers continued their gentle massage. 'Leo must be quite a guy.'

She nodded, turning her hand and lacing their fingers together. 'Was,' she said gently. 'He died in February. He was only in his fifties, but he had a heart attack and that was—— He knew he had a problem. The doctors were trying to schedule him for surgery and he was stalling.'

He let her be quiet for a long time before he said, 'Tell me about when you called Leo.'

She didn't think she had told him. He must have guessed. She supposed it wouldn't have been hard to guess. 'I didn't call him for a year, but I didn't do anything with the phone number. I kept it,

memorised it actually. I thought about it sometimes
. . . thought about it a lot, but . . .'

The music came up to a crashing climax, then
faded away to nothing. They sat quietly with the
sounds of the water moving gently against the hull,
voices somewhere nearby, perhaps on one of the
other boats.

'Just say it,' Joe said in a low voice. 'Something
happened. Someone hurt you. That was what finally
got you to call Leo.'

'It wasn't really that big a deal,' she said finally. 'I
was out walking on the beach. It was night and I
was thinking, wondering how long the commune
thing would last before I had to move out, wondering
where I would go. I thought of Leo, but I couldn't
have gone back to another foster home. I was sixteen
and that was what would have happened if I'd gone
to a social worker for help. Another foster home.
Then—I didn't see him at first, but there was this
kid. If I'd seen, I would have given him a wide berth.
I wasn't stupid, and staying untouched through that
year took more than just luck. There were times—
Well, I just didn't want anyone to force me into
anything, whether it was a foster home or sex.'

She shook her head, although he hadn't said
anything. 'I don't have to say it, do I? He was young,
I guess about my age. He was ridiculously strong,
because I don't think he was any taller than I was. I
gave him a hell of a fight, and in the end I hurt him
worse than he hurt me. He got a broken arm. All I
got was just—just a memory. It was no big deal.'

She felt the anger in him, knew without his words
that he wanted to have hold of that poor kid who
had taken her all those years ago. 'It's so far back

that I—— It didn't really happen to me. It was another girl. And it was the thing that made me phone Leo. I ran up and called an ambulance for the kid. Then I hid until it came. I could feel the dark and the—there was nothing for me there. I'd be a scared kid on the beach forever if I didn't do something about it. When the ambulance had gone, I came up and . . .' she shook her hair back as if to shed the past '. . . and called Leo.'

He said dully, 'When I was sixteen, I went to air-cadet camp.' He closed his eyes and said, 'I was two days on the train, alone. For God's sake, Dinah, it was the first time I ever travelled alone!'

She smiled and found his cheek with her lips. Her chair scraped on the deck and she felt his cool, hard flesh under her lips. 'You're a nice man, Joe. Don't worry about the old me. After all, I've got a house and a steady job. And you—you're bumming around the world without a home.' He wouldn't smile. She said, 'It's happened to a lot of women, you know. It's not the end of the world unless you let it be. I'm sane and not all that hung up about it. I—I had an affair afterwards, so you see, I'm not——'

'Why?' he asked softly. 'To prove you weren't afraid of sex?'

He could see a lot more than she had intended, or had she said more than she'd meant to? 'If so, I proved it.'

'And how was it?' he asked gently.

'Disappointing.' She drew away.

'And you haven't tried again?' He frowned. 'When——?'

'Six years.' She had been twenty, and maybe she had proved something, but if so it didn't need proving more than once. 'If I do it again, it'll be because I want to. It'll be . . .' For love, but she must not tell him that.

He stood up and the violence in him was not nearly as controlled as she had thought. 'I don't know what—I hate to think of—— Damn it, Dinah! I've got a pretty fierce urge to kill that bit of slime!'

For some odd reason that made her smile. She joined him, touched his shoulder fleetingly. 'Does it occur to you that that's a funny urge for a man who doesn't want to get involved?'

'Yeah,' he agreed. She heard him swallow. 'I'm involved, all right. You'd think I was a Mexican, the way you tie me in knots. I don't know where the hell it's going, but . . .' He closed his eyes and she found her hands touching his face. She felt a shudder go through him and he groaned, 'I'd better take you back. You'd better get the hell out of here.'

It was an ache in her, the loving. He felt it, too, although perhaps he had to pretend to himself that it was only a physical thing. He was afraid to touch her, afraid of where it would lead him. She touched him, felt again his trembling, and knew that she would love him long after he had sailed away.

He was a man who would go away, and she was a woman who needed roots. But she loved him, and it would not pass easily. She knew from his eyes that she could not tell him, but she was not going to walk away from it either. If Leo had taught her anything, it was that love was always worth the pain.

CHAPTER SEVEN

'HEY, *Free Moments*! Anybody aboard?'

Dinah jerked and Joe turned away from her. 'Hello, who's that?' Joe's voice showed his relief at the interruption. A head appeared on the far side of the boat, eyes peering up over the rail. 'Hi, Walt. I didn't know you were in harbour. Come on aboard.'

'No, thanks.' Walt's voice sounded tired. 'I just got into port today, want to get back to the boat and have a good sleep.' His eyes took in the shadow that was Dinah on the deck. Joe made no move to introduce her. Walt said, 'I was checking in at the port captain's earlier. I ran into Lucie. She said you were looking for a girl. Gringo girl. Pregnant.' His voice shifted to a question. 'Very pregnant? Redhead, round face?'

Dinah's head jerked. 'Cathy! Was her name Cathy?'

Walt's eyes shifted. Joe said, 'This is Dinah. She's looking for Cathy.'

'Hi, Dinah. I dunno about the name. She was up at San Francisco, on *Buena Vista*. All I knew is she wasn't Barry's regular crew. He's single-handing—at least, he was. So he got the pregnant girl from somewhere. I saw them on the beach, said hello, but you know how it is, Joe. Barry and I aren't buddies. We didn't get to names.'

'Sure.' Joe was looking down, relaxed against the safety rail. 'You won't have a beer, Walt?' Walt hesitated and Joe said, 'Come aboard. I'll get it.'

Walt fiddled with the rope to his dinghy, and got it tied. Then Joe called up from below, 'Tie your dinghy behind my rubber one, would you? That way it won't bang into the boat.

Walt shrugged, grinned at Dinah and untied the rope, taking it to the back of the boat to refasten it. Then he came back to sit in the chair beside Dinah.

He greeted the beer with enthusiasm. Joe sat on the anchor winch with his own beer and asked, 'Tell me about Barry. I've never run across him.'

Walt settled deeper into the chair. 'Young guy. Twenties. Early twenties, I guess.' He scowled and complained, 'Where do these guys get the money to go cruising? The rest of us work away, wait and save, and—— He seems an OK guy. He's got a twenty-four-foot Dana. Nice little boat. Crowded for two people, though, I guess. I dunno if she's a permanent fixture or just visiting. You know? You don't ask that sort of thing.'

'Sure,' agreed Joe easily. 'Where's he going? Do you know?'

'More or less.'

Dinah listened, getting a glimpse at the kind of society these people had. Meeting again and again, often knowing little about each other, not asking last names or personal questions, but talking about boats and future plans and storms that had been weathered.

Walt took a long drink of his beer and said, 'They were in San Francisco last—well, night before last. Not talking about pulling up the hook yet, but you know how it is. Barry talked about further up the sea. Escondido. Bahia de la Concepción. No hurry, just working their way up. I wondered about the girl. She didn't look like she had long to go, and the medicos up that way aren't too fluent in English. I'd have thought they'd be better here until—well, maybe she wasn't staying. He didn't really say.'

'San Francisco?' Dinah had realised by this time that they weren't talking about the city of the Golden Gate bridge. 'Is it far?'

'A day's travel,' answered Joe, adding, 'By boat. It's an island. We'll head over there in the morning.'

She looked up at his mast, at the radar dome on the front of it. 'Can't we start now? You've got radar, and——'

'No way.' His voice was sharp, definite. 'I've been drinking, and I'm not going to add to the tales of idiots going aground getting in and out of La Paz bay. In any case, we can't.'

Walt said, 'Port captain,' and Joe explained to Dinah.

'We're foreigners. This is a foreign vessel. We can't just roam around at will. I've got to go up to the port captain and file a crew list and destination.'

'*Aguas de la jurisdicción*,' murmured Walt.

'What?' Dinah asked, and Joe smiled.

'Sorry, *señorita*. We mix up Spanish and English as if they were one language, don't we? But I think I'd better file a crew list for Escondido, just in case we go further afield. If Barry has moved on, we could end up trailing Cathy all the way to Escondido. Best to be prepared for that.'

When Walt left, Joe ran Dinah back to shore in the dinghy, stayed to flag her a taxi and made the bargain with the driver, setting the price for the ride back to the hotel.

'Pack a bathing suit if you have one,' he suggested. 'And trousers, but those loose dresses, too. It's hot out there, and for heaven's sake bring your sun-screen.' He frowned, and said, 'It's ridiculous for you to pay for that hotel. We may be gone days. Throw what you don't want for the boat into your car and check out. I'll meet you at eight in the morning and we'll do the paperwork.'

He lifted a hand in the half wave and the driver started the taxi moving. Dinah wondered why she hadn't had the nerve to reach out and touch his face, invite the kiss she wanted.

Joe shouted and the driver braked violently. Dinah twisted around to see what was wrong, and found Joe leaning in her open window. He touched her cheek gently and she felt her breath catch in her throat. He bent and touched his lips to hers, whispered to her.

'Dinah, *señorita*, I need one more of your secrets.'

'What? Now?' With the taxi-driver watching, grinning?

'Your last name. I need it for the crew list.'

'Oh.' She covered her disappointment. For heaven's sake, what had she thought he wanted? 'It's Collins. Dinah Collins.'

Joe picked her up the next morning and they started the rounds of smiling officials. First to the immigration office where the official checked her tourist permit and Joe's, then stamped Joe's crew list for departure. Then to the port captain almost two miles away. More stamps. The crew list was beginning to look like quite an official document, covered with the blue and black ink of rubber stamps. They left copies everywhere.

Finally they were free to leave. It was eleven in the morning by this time. 'What do you do with the three copies you've got left?' Dinah asked, as they motored out to the sailboat in Joe's dinghy.

'Need them when we get back. Another whole round of everybody. Actually, if I'd just cleared for the surrounding area, I wouldn't have had to do all this. Just the port captain then.'

As they went out to the boat, Joe seemed to become more talkative, as if a weight were coming off him. As they were motoring out of the harbour, he invited her to help him handle sail. It was fun, getting the sail up under the hot sun, feeling it fill with the breeze, *Free Moments* leaning into the wind and slipping through the water.

'Pull that silver button,' he instructed her. He was standing on the lazarette hatch, adjusting the wind-vane that would self-steer the boat while they were sailing. He gestured with his free hand, his other arm holding the safety rail for support.

When she slid out the button, silence flowed over them. Silence, then slowly sounds filling it. The gentle slap of water on the hull, the sound of the wind on the Canadian flag at the back of the boat. Magic, she decided, watching Joe go forward to adjust the mains'l.

'This is not a fast way to do it,' he told her with a smile. He was standing with his legs astride on the cabin top, winching a halyard tighter. She loved the hard, strong motion of his sailor's muscles. 'Let loose that line—yeah, that one. Good, now pull it in until—that's it!' The mains'l was smooth now, the wind curving along its wing-shaped profile. 'We'd go faster under engine power with so little wind, but we can't make Isla San Francisco before dark in any case. We'll stop at Partida for the night.' He stepped down, grinning at her. 'If you want a beautiful ride, something special, go up front.'

'Up on the foredeck?' The ride was already beautiful. It had the floating freedom of a dancer with magic music.

'Further.' He smiled into the dreamy light in her eyes, touched her hair to brush it back against the wind. 'Right up on the bow pulpit.' She threw an uneasy glance forward and he said, 'It's safe. The rails are high, and once you're out there you can sit down on the lower rail and it's like a free circus ride. Safer, though.'

'Safer?' She wasn't sure.

'Coward?' He was laughing, his eyes a brilliant blue like the sky overhead, the water around. 'You'll drive down the Baja, but you hesitate to sit in my bow pulpit?' He leaned close, brushed her lips with a soft, highly charged caress. 'The water's warm, *señorita*. If you fall in, I'll come back for you.'

As he had promised, it was a magic place. Way up front, past the narrow gap between the jib sail and the bow pulpit. She was wearing a blue blouse and skirt that she had found in the market a couple of days ago and been unable to resist. She hardly ever wore dresses at home, but in this heat the loose cottons were irresistible. And Joe's eyes when he looked at her in a swirling skirt . . .

She held the skirt bunched to one side as she climbed out. She ended up sitting at the very front of the bowsprit, seat on the rail and back supported by the upper rail. A secure seat, the bowsprit below a stable grip for her feet. She closed her eyes, felt the surging rush of water below, looked down and felt the power of this vessel surging through the sea, the white foam of the ocean boiling up around the bow.

Looking towards the stern, she could see the whole boat, its shape a gentle invasion of the water, the blue streaming out behind. Joe at the wheel, grinning at her, waving and shouting. She could not hear his words for the sound of the water below her. What an exciting, fast ride, sitting out over the boiling water, aware of the violent peace of the boat's passage, yet so safe on her perch!

There was a fascinating intimacy in the way he signalled to her when he went below. It was noisy up here and his voice would not carry to her, but his hand moved and he smiled. A sound barrier that words could not penetrate. As if they were suspended in another dimension, isolated from the world as well as the medium of talking.

Cathy, she thought, but there was nothing she could do about Cathy until they caught up with the boat *Buena Vista*. Meanwhile, she had a holiday, a gift of fate in the midst of her search for Leo's charge.

Joe brought out a tray filled with something that looked good. He shouted and she could not hear, but he waved and she came. Away from the bow, the noise of sailing became very gentle. They sat cross-legged on the fore deck and ate cheese and tortillas while the wind-vane kept the sailboat on course. Then Joe got a rope and a bucket and dipped up warm sea water. 'For dessert,' he told her with a grin, pulling out a pocket-knife and hacking away at the mangoes he had brought up from below.

'You're not doing that very delicately,' Dinah

teased him as she accepted a messy piece of the sweet fruit.

'There's no delicate way to eat mangoes,' he mumbled around a mouthful. 'You just have to do it next to a good supply of water.'

'The knife's not sharp,' she insisted, taking it from the deck and attacking another mango. The slippery fruit eluded her attempts to cut it tidily.

'It's sharp.' He rinsed his fingers and took her wrist in his hand, drawing it to his lips. She gasped as he took her index finger into his mouth, sucking the sweet juice. 'Good,' he murmured, but she could feel the shaken quality in his voice. It was nothing to what her own wild heart was doing.

He let her hand go and she rinsed her fingers, but when she bent over the fruit again her hand was too unsteady to dare picking up the knife. 'It's your knife,' she managed lightly. 'You cut the mango. After all, we're in the land of *machismo*, aren't we? And surely the knifework should be the man's job.'

It was achingly sweet to take the warm, juicy fruit from his fingers, to put it in her teeth and find her lips closing around his thumb, feeling the ridge of his thumbnail biting into her lower lip. His eyes were immersed deep into hers. There was no touch except his thumb between her lips, his finger lying against her cheek.

A low groan came from his throat before she realised that she was sucking, drawing his thumb into her mouth in a sensuous caress. Her tongue touched, caressed, then she drew back and his hand was free, her eyes wide and heart wild.

'I—I'm—sorry.' Was that breathless whisper her voice?

'Are you?' His chest was rising and falling rapidly, his breathing irregular. She saw his chest expand in a deep, shaggy breath before he announced unsteadily, 'We're becalmed.'

'What?' His face was smooth and relaxed, his lips parted as if . . . 'We're what?'

'No wind.' He pushed the tray away. There was only Joe and the warm gloss of the teak deck, the caress of the sun. He breathed, 'Sails are slack.'

He touched her jaw and somehow her head was rocking back, her eyes taking in the folds of the drooping sail. 'Joe?' she whispered, and his hand was at the back of her head, supporting it, the blonde glossy hair filtering through his fingers. She swallowed and her eyes had trouble watching him, seeing the way his gaze was drawn to her throat as it moved in a spasm she could not put a name to.

'Will the wind come back?' God! She sounded scared, young. There was nothing to hide what was inside her from those eyes.

Something happened in his eyes. He shifted, leaned and she was gently lowered to the warm deck, his fingers smoothing her hair out over the warm teak. 'Not . . . not for a while.' He was having trouble talking, too. Heat, the fierce sun of the tropics welling up between them, no words but only the aching, sweet desire, the closeness that did not need a touch, that waited for loving.

I love you. It was in her eyes, a deep pressure in her chest. His head blocked out most of the sky, his fingers trailing along the embroidered edge of her blouse near her shoulder. The blouse was fastened at the front by a series of little ties, bows running down from the swelling above her breasts to her waist. She felt his eyes slowly unfastening the bows and she forgot to breathe.

'Dinah ...' It was a breath of wind, perhaps, except the air was still. Below the blouse was a matching tiered skirt of the gauzy material popular with the Mexican women in summer. All morning she had been catching the skirt, holding it against the wind. Now the air was still and the skirt lay around her legs in a sensuous disarray. His eyes had watched, and she admitted to herself that she had not changed into more practical jeans because ... because she wanted that look in his eyes, craved it and needed it.

'The wind?' Her tongue slipped out to moisten dry lips. Behind his head was the white of the sail, a darker stain on the fabric from its years of use. She looked at his face, his brows hunched together slightly, eyes taking her insides apart in a conquest that had nothing to do with her body, yet everything. 'Will the wind come back?'

He caught the end of one of the little ties with his thumb and index finger. His other arm supported his body as he leaned over her, only the backs of his fingers brushing as he slowly pulled the bow open. As the two halves of the top bow drew apart, he pulled gently and the blouse parted slightly, revealing the sun-browned swelling that led further, to the whiteness that had not been touched by the sun.

'All day,' he whispered raggedly, 'it's been driving me insane.' He pulled another tie, slowly, so slowly, and this time the weight of her released breasts pulled the fabric apart. He swallowed. 'I knew you weren't wearing a bra.'

She pulled in a hot lungful of air. Without the wind, the air was hot. It seemed to fill her breast, expanding, and she felt the fabric part more, felt a wonderful excitement at the way his blue eyes turned black on her. She said raggedly, 'It's too hot for a bra. I need all the air movement on—all the . . .'

He pulled another tie, but this time his fingers were trembling and she could feel the shudder of his hand against the flesh of her midriff. Slowly, another tie. And another. Then there was nothing holding the two sides of her bodice together. The lacy cotton lay barely covering the peaks of her breasts. Below the blouse, his eyes tangled with the elastic waistband of her skirt as it caressed her, almost concealing her navel.

His fingers possessed the edge of her blouse just a breath away from the undersurface of her breasts, then stilled. His chest stilled too, only his eyes moving as they explored the warm white line of her flesh, the relaxed cleavage of her breasts disappearing in two womanly curves under the blouse. The soft tenderness of her midriff.

'I can see your nipples,' he groaned, and she felt her nipples rising to his words, thrusting against the thin blue fabric of the blouse. 'All day, when I looked at you, and . . .' His eyes closed, painfully, briefly. She saw his throat work. 'I could see you wanting me.'

There was no doubt of how he wanted her. His jeans could not conceal his need. His eyes said more than his lips ever would. She felt a sharp pain, the foreknowledge that there would never be another day as sweet as this one. Then her fingers lifted and tangled in the fine, stiff hairs of his chest. She felt his jerk as her palm brushed through the tangle of hair, caressing the hard erection of his male nipple.

'Joe . . . I'm not very used to . . . I——'

'I know.' His chest seemed to cave in, the air from his lungs expelled in an uncontrolled blast. She felt his fingers curl on the edge of her blouse, the hardness of his knuckles digging faintly into her midriff. 'Dinah, I . . .' His touch lightened, drawing one side of her blouse open. The sun caressed her breast, the hard, turgid peak of her nipple. 'You . . .' She saw a shudder go through his body, then his hand possessed her breast, a gentle touch that asked nothing, cupping and holding, no more.

The world was still, Joe's face vulnerable and open as it had never been before. Dinah could feel herself spread out below him, her arm flung wide, her hair a sensuous maze on the deck, her skirt a wild invitation.

'The wind won't come up for a while. It's the still, hot part of the day.' His voice sounded almost normal, but she could see his eyes, the heaving of his chest under the mat of his hair. Slowly, in his eyes, she saw his emotions come under his control until she could feel nothing of what was inside him, only her own need, her own vulnerability.

Could he see the love in her eyes? She knew that he was going to draw back. His fingers released her breast without the beginning of the sensuous caress that had been advertised in his eyes a moment ago.

He was afraid. She could feel it, knew the reason because it was in her too. Their touch went too deep, was more than the mere physical. She whispered, 'Joe, when did you——? Has there been anyone since . . .?'

Since his wife. No. She knew the answer. It was there, hidden by his eyes. He said in a low voice, 'Why should I——?' She didn't know what he had meant to say, but he shook his head and he was drawing back.

She closed her fingers on the other side of her blouse, drew it open and felt the sun everywhere, warming. 'Please,' she said carefully, but her love was there in her voice no matter what she tried to hide it with. She whispered, 'Joe?' and she would have thought from the hardness of his face that he was not moved by the warm softness of her woman's breast, except that his eyes turned black.

'I've been frozen,' he said harshly. His eyes closed, opened again before the lashes could touch his cheek. 'You . . . I—ever since I first saw you, you've been like that damned sun melting the ice and—Dinah, I——' His fists clenched, then opened, and he said dully, 'I'm not—I can't promise anything.'

'No promises,' she said softly. She loved him so much, needed to take the cold core of his loneliness and warm it up with her love. It was not possible for her to turn away, to close herself from the wonderful warmth of loving this man. 'No promises. I'm not asking you for anything except . . . just now . . . today.' Then his head descended, his lips tasting her sweetness and drawing back, his eyes touching the warm curves of her breasts. 'I wouldn't want you to get sunburn,' he said raggedly, and his mouth took sweetness from the slope that led to one hardened peak of her arousal while his head shadowed and protected her from the sun.

She found the sun-bleached wildness of his hair and her fingers tangled in it, drawing his lips to hers, tightening as her lips parted and his tongue possessed the dark, sensitive secrets of her kiss.

'One promise,' he said, and his voice was sure and deep. The trembling of his hands was gone as he pushed the blouse from her shoulder and kissed the hollow that was exposed, drew up to explore the line from shoulder to breastbone where her tan ended. 'The sun wanted to kiss you like this,' he said huskily, his mouth moving on to the whiteness, his lips against her skin as the words passed. 'It will be good for you. I promise you that, *señorita*.'

He kissed her eyes. She smiled and something inside wanted to cry, but there was no pain, only joy. She looked, saw his lips curved in a smile, and even if he turned away tomorrow she would know that there had been love in his eyes. 'I keep my promises,' he said softly. 'And I promise you won't think it's overrated this time.'

Her voice teased unsteadily, 'Are you that good? Or is it that Mexican *machismo*? I guess it is catching.' His lips descended along the slope of her breast and she lost her breath, then gasped, although his kiss had not reached her nipple yet.

She felt his hot breath on her nipple, felt her breast tremble with aching fullness. His voice growled. *'We're* that good.' His lips touched, just barely touched the hard peak. Her fingers clenched in his hair, her body twisting, seeking closeness. 'You know that we're that good.'

Words, she thought, as he drew back again. He was going to destroy her with waiting, with words that excited her as much as touches. She could feel the pressure building, a need she had never experienced before. Her hands slipped to his shoulders, explored the bunched muscles, the smooth planes that were hardness and satiny smoothness, the soft cushion of his chest pelt.

'Then do something about it,' she urged, shameless now.

His fingers trailed from her shoulder to her waist, feeling the swellings, the hollows, the trembling. 'Slower is better,' he murmured, his fingers tracing the line of her hip, her thigh through the skirt. 'I love to see the sun on you. There's a sail over there.' His eyes grazed past her breasts, over the glistening, quiet water. 'Miles away,' he said softly. 'He has no idea that we aren't just sitting here fishing.'

His eyes came back then. Her fingers curled around his shoulders, found that she was not strong enough to pull him down to her. She drew herself up into his arms, against his chest. He smoothed the blouse down over her shoulders, away from them, and his arms were hard against her smooth back, drawing her close, her skirt tangled around his legs as he bent his head and took her lips in a hard kiss that lasted forever.

They were both trembling when he lifted his head. She pulled closer, if it were possible, felt the hard curve of his male breast crushing her softness.

'Dinah . . .'

'You're not going to tell me that you're not prepared for this?' She swallowed.

'No,' he growled, and she felt his laugh. 'You won't catch me twice that way.' Then something went molten in his eyes and she found herself spread out on the deck, his hard body following her own, his lips tracing all the curves, his hands smoothing the barriers away.

And then it was her lips, her hands. His ragged jeans giving way to her fumbling exploration. Her gauzy skirt. Her lacy briefs. His leg, hard and exciting, parting hers.

The sky spinning. The sound from her lips, from deep inside her. A groan, like a wild thing. Then her body too, driven wild by caresses she had not dreamed of. His lips everywhere, the salty taste of his shoulder under her mouth, the hard ridge of his abdomen.

Then a pause, the trembling of his hands as he did what was needed to protect her. His hands and his lips, his body taking hers, his tongue probing for the source of the shuddering cry from her throat. She thought the world exploded, the sun ignited in a hot fire that would burn forever, hotter and hotter and hotter.

Deep inside, the pressure welled up. The sun. The man. The thrusting rhythm that was taking her apart, driving her to a wild need beyond living, beyond loving, beyond . . .

She heard her own cry from a long way off, then, while she was still trembling, her throat sending out soft, husky sounds of a fulfilled ecstasy, she felt his explosive release. His arms gripped her hard, everything rigid, still for a timeless instant, then one final thrust sent his body into a shuddering spasm that left him spent in her arms.

CHAPTER EIGHT

DINAH felt Joe's withdrawal. His arms were still around her, his head buried in her breast, his eyes closed.

At first she thought he was sleeping. She was drifting on the tide that was the aftermath of their loving, feeling the warm weight of his body as it lay on hers. His breathing steadied, became slow and deep. She felt every breath of his through her body, felt the hard beat of his heart as it slowed to normal. Overhead, the sky was bright, the sun hot. She closed her eyes and let the feelings overwhelm her. This would be forever, waking with his body against hers, moments alone knowing that later Joe would be there.

Always . . . forever. Never again the cold certainty that she was alone in the world. Loving made them one. Home. Children. Forever.

Somewhere in the dreaming that seemed real she felt the tension jerk into his body, as if he had caught her dreams and rejected them. Then he was withdrawing. A moment's stillness, then his weight leaving her, his body turning as it rose.

He did not want to look into her eyes.

He pushed back his hair, stood up, looking out over the water, away from her. She could feel that he was searching for words, but he had already said the words. No promises. No future. She had been wrong, thinking that the joy would be more than the pain. It was going to tear her apart. He was going to walk away from her, wanted right now to run away, and that was going to be worse than anything that had gone before.

She was naked, her clothes a jumble somewhere on the deck. She said tightly, 'The boat's not moving, is it?' She didn't wait for an answer, but said quickly, 'I think I'll go for a swim.'

She dived quickly, the water closing around her body with a shock that felt cool for only a second. Then she swam, hard, feeling the water slip along her bare skin, a sensuous pleasure that she had never experienced before.

She circled the boat twice, then came to rest lying on her back, floating gently on the water. She could not see Joe, didn't know where he was. She closed her eyes and felt the sun, the water, and tried to feel calm enough to know how she could face him again.

Then his hand closed on her shoulder and she gasped and foundered in the water, taking in a mouthful of salt water and choking. His hands pulled her upright, his arms catching under hers, drawing her close.

'Sorry, *señorita*.' She felt her body drifting towards his, her breasts floating up against his chest. 'You float more easily than me,' he said raggedly. 'You have these flotation chambers . . .' His eyes were on the roundness that was uplifted by the water.

'I don't need a bra with water-uplift like that,' she said breathlessly. There was no laughter in his eyes, they were black and disturbed. She swallowed. 'Joe, I—— It was just going to be—— It isn't so simple, is it?' Making love, but it meant loving, too.

He shook his head, his arms releasing her. They floated, facing each other, a couple of feet between them. 'We'd better get on our way,' he said finally.

'We've got to get to an anchorage. We—I—Dinah, I didn't mean to do anything to hurt you.'

She saw it in his eyes. He could see what was in her heart. Had she cried out her love when he'd been teaching her that a man and a woman together could be heaven?

She licked her lips, said quietly, 'Joe, I love you.' The breath left his lungs as if someone had hit him with a hard fist and she said quickly, 'I don't expect anything. I—I just wanted you to know.'

'Dinah——' He swallowed, and said grimly, 'I shouldn't have let this happen. You—I haven't got anything to give.'

'Haven't you?' His eyes darkened and she whispered, 'I think you have, Joe. I think it's there, and if you let yourself you could love me as much as—I think you're afraid to.'

He seemed to spend the rest of the day trying to pretend that their loving had not happened. He dressed quickly, got the boat under way under engine power while she was dressing inside. Then he put them on autopilot, asked her to watch for other boats, and went below to organise a meal in the galley.

'Partida anchorage,' he announced when he had set the anchor some hours later. They were in a bay formed by the joining of two islands and Joe insisted that they take the dinghy ashore to explore. She thought it was a way to stop him from being alone with her, sitting doing nothing and taking the chance that the closeness would overcome them again.

There was a small settlement of Mexican fishermen on the beach, living in shacks built from tar paper, cardboard and driftwood. Joe lifted a hand in greeting and walked towards one of the Mexicans.

He said, '*Hola. Como está?*' and the two men were off in a stream of social chit-chat that Dinah could not understand. She caught the word '*playa*' and knew that was beach, but the rest of it was gibberish to her. She wandered away along the flat, hard-packed sand, discarding her shoes and making easier progress in bare feet.

She was sitting cross-legged, sifting sand through her fingers, when he came walking slowly down the beach to her. He dropped down beside her and leaned back, looking past her towards the shacks, the volleyball-court rigged in the sand outside them.

'Joe, would you tell me about your wife?'

She saw him take a deep breath as if he was going to shut her out, then he shrugged. 'I got married while I was still in medical school.' His eyes found hers. She could not read anything in them. She wanted to touch him, but she thought he would stop talking if she did.

'Julie. Her family lived two doors down from ours. She was younger, played with my kid brothers. When I was at college, I came home for holidays, we'd talk . . . about her skinned knees . . . about whether she'd pass algebra. The year before I graduated she finished business college and got a job in Vancouver, in the West End. I was at UBC medical school. We started going out and . . .'

He drew a line in the sand with his fingers. His voice was toneless. 'We got married at Christmas, kind of shocked both our parents. Mine especially, because Dad was opposed to a doctor taking on responsibilities before he was able to make a living.'

A *ponga* roared as it came into the bay. Joe watched as it sped towards the shore, saw the Mexican driver give the engine a final burst to send the boat right up on to the beach a few hundred yards away. Joe wiped something from his forehead that she couldn't see, and said, 'She kept on working until I finished my residency. When I was established in a practice in Victoria, she quit work.'

Another boat followed the first. Someone laughed, and the sound came to them across the sand. 'We had two kids. Sherrie and Bruce. It was all so easy.' He spread his hands, seeing Dinah now and asking something with his eyes that she couldn't answer. 'Maybe it was too easy,' he said finally. 'I had it all and I really hadn't done anything to earn it. She was so damned young. And the kids. Sherrie was blonde and plump. She grinned easily.' He smiled, looking back at his daughter. 'Bruce was eighteen months. He had dark curly hair like Julie. He was just starting to talk.'

When the silence stretched too tight, she said, 'Was?' and braced herself because it was in his eyes. She wanted to tell him that they could have children, but knew you could not replace people that were gone.

He shook his head, but the memory didn't leave his eyes. 'I was driving. I wasn't speeding. I never did. I'd seen too much at the hospital, too many reasons not to be in a hurry behind the wheel. We were on our way home after a weekend trip to Vancouver. The kids were in the back. Julie had taken off her seat-belt and was curled up in the front seat, half asleep.' His voice was toneless, like a reporter reading from paper. 'An eighteen-wheel tractor-trailer rig went out of control and crossed the highway straight for me.' He shrugged and lost some of the mask. 'It wasn't his fault either. Some mechanical failure. I didn't really listen to the explanation when I heard it, and now——' He pushed his hair back and said with low impatience, 'Anyway, that was it. I woke up in hospital. I was the only one to survive.'

She leaned across and found his hand. It turned and gripped hers. He said tonelessly, 'I got out of the hospital. There was the funeral . . . then two weeks more getting my body in shape to go back to work. Hank was on me, telling me to take more time off, but I had to get back to work. It seemed the only thing in my life worth doing.'

She said, 'I understand,' and his fingers closed on hers.

'I don't know if I do. Back at work I went around for two weeks like a zombie. I hope I was some use to my patients.' He drew in a deep breath. 'The second week, I had an emergency delivery. She'd been my patient through four miscarriages, and she was working like hell to make this one work. She was almost due, and when things started going haywire I had an anaesthetist ready and we did a Caesarean. I'd talked it over with her first, and she knew that I wasn't going to take any chances with her history.'

He withdrew his hand and she asked, 'What happened?'

'Everything went fine. I delivered her. It was a boy, big enough and healthy, although of course he was born under anaesthetic. I closed her up and then she just went.' He said harshly, 'She died. There was an autopsy, of course, and it wasn't anything that had happened in surgery. She had a brain tumour that no one suspected, that there was no reason to suspect.' He shrugged. 'Then—I don't know, everything just seemed to fall apart. Julie and the kids, and this woman. They'd all been in my care, and somehow I hadn't managed to hold on to any of them, to——'

She got on to her knees and went to him, her hands against his chest. 'Joe, you know that's not rational. You must know that.'

'Oh, I know it.' He said wryly, 'Hank spent a lot of time telling me what it was in fancy words. The only thing he said, though, that really made any sense to me, was that I should get the hell away. It seemed like a good idea, and I did it. I arranged for another doctor to take over my patients for three months and I went.'

'Three years ago? On the boat?' She stroked his arm where it rested on the chair, but he didn't feel it.

'Yes. Julie and I bought the boat the year after Sherrie was born. Julie named it. *Free Moments*, because I didn't have that many. I should have taken it easier, given her more time . . . the kids.'

She said softly, 'Three years ago? You can't stay away forever.'

He drew back and she was alone, although there were only inches between them. 'Yes, I can,' he said harshly.

Of course he could. She nodded, and said, 'You can sail away and just keep going?' Living in this country was very inexpensive and she supposed whatever savings he had would last a long time. But . . . 'It's not the right thing,' she said softly. 'I know you have to make your own decisions, but Joe—I know about this. I've lost everybody that ever mattered to me. My parents. Leo. But if you turn away from people, don't let yourself get involved—well, maybe you don't get hurt, but you sure the hell don't live either.'

Her heart was pounding and he was not going to say anything. She said raggedly, 'I'm sorry. It's none of my business, is it?'

'No,' he agreed, standing up, shaking her words off. 'Let's go back to the boat. We'll get an early start tomorrow.' But he was the one who stood still, not moving, staring out at his own boat. Finally he moved, saying briskly, 'We've got to find Cathy. That's what you came to Mexico for.'

Did he still love Julie?

That night as Dinah slept in the small cabin at the front of the boat she found that she could lie very still and hear Joe's breathing. Maybe that was symbolic of what was between them. Dinah alone in a bunk, awake, listening. Joe, sleeping in the next cabin, his life not altered by the woman who loved him. But his touch on her body and her soul had altered her world forever.

The next day was windy and they had hard work sailing north to Isla San Francisco. The wind was brisk from the north. Joe set the sails and tacked into the waves and wind, beating their way slowly towards the island in jagged steps dictated by the strong northerly.

Joe called it sailing uphill, going against the wind. It was wet, the bow of the boat pounding into the waves, sending sheets of spray back over the cockpit. With the sun overhead, the wind and waves wild, the hard work of hauling on lines and winches seemed to fill her with a new energy.

They were too busy handling the boat to feel tension between them. Dinah found Joe easy to work with, his instructions clear and calm. He didn't shout or get excited, but when the boat leaned over hard and pounded into the white water she could see the grin of pleasure on his face and she felt happy. Maybe Alice could be talked into giving up her crew position. Maybe Joe would let Dinah come with him if she didn't talk about loving.

The tiny Isla San Francisco grew larger on the horizon. It was a small island with a crescent-shaped bay on its west side. It was late afternoon before they rounded the lighthouse at the entrance to the bay and escaped the wild water by motoring over to the north side.

There were three other boats anchored in the bay, all sailboats. 'Don't recognise any of them,' said Joe tersely, as he went forward to let the anchor go. 'Wait till we get settled, then we'll see.'

The anchor made a thump, then a rumbling race of chain. Joe took his time after the anchor was set, watching the rocks on the beach, judging whether they were solidly anchored. 'If the wind turns south,' he warned her, 'we'll have to set to and move over to the other side of the bay. This is a beautiful spot, but it's not much of an anchorage in a south wind.'

The boat closest to the shore was *Buena Vista*. 'Do you want me to go with you?' asked Joe. 'Or would it be better for you to see her alone?'

'I don't know.' Now, so close to Cathy, she was aware of all the things that could go wrong. Cathy had written to Leo, might not welcome Dinah's appearance in his place. What if it wasn't Cathy, after all? 'I need you,' she said finally. 'For the dinghy. I don't know how to run it.'

He nodded and started readying the dinghy, adding wryly, 'And for courage?' and she admitted that he was right.

'I'm nervous about how she'll react. She wrote to Leo, and—well, she called for help. I just have to hope she'll accept it from me.'

'She might not need it,' Joe pointed out, as he held the dinghy for her to board. 'She might have worked it out for herself.'

'Worked it out?' Dinah forced her voice calm. 'Joe, she's just a kid. Do you think she'll make it, hopping from man to man for a bread ticket?'

He shook his head. 'No. I'm sorry. Let's go.' He fired the dinghy engine up and they started out, and she thought he murmured something like, 'I just hope we don't have trouble with the captain of the bloody boat.'

Dinah hadn't really thought of all this from the point of view of the man on *Buena Vista*.

A few minutes later they learned that he looked even younger than Walt had suggested. His head appeared through a hatch when Joe rapped on the hull of the boat. He was frowning, annoyed at the interruption. Dinah guessed he was about twenty-two.

Joe said, 'We're looking for a Canadian girl named Cathy Stinardson.'

If it were possible, Barry scowled more deeply. 'Why? Who are you?'

'Friends,' Dinah said quickly. 'She is here, isn't she? She wrote, and—'

'She wrote to her friend Leo.' The boy was scowling and Dinah had the feeling that he had problems deeper than he was able to handle.

'I know,' she said.

Joe said mildly, 'Look, why not let us come on board? I'm Joe and this is Dinah, and we're not going to do either you or Cathy any harm. You're Barry, aren't you?'

'Yeah.' He hesitated, then nodded. 'OK. She's inside. She's not feeling very good.' As Dinah climbed on to the boat, Barry asked, 'Is there really a guy called Leo? I wasn't sure if she was having me on or not.'

Joe caught Dinah's hand as she started into the cabin. 'I'll wait here. It's going to be easier for her if there aren't too many of us. Call me if you need me.'

'Thanks.' She smiled at the warmth in his eyes and inside her something began to flower. This man was going to have a hard time keeping the indifferent mask he had sported when she'd first met him. She said softly, 'I know I can count on you,' and he looked startled, but not as alarmed as he might have a few days ago.

Cathy had not had the baby yet, but it couldn't be long now. She was lying on the settee behind a dining table, her Mexican-style summer dress stretched enormously over the abdomen. When she saw Dinah she did not recognise her.

'Barry,' she said uneasily, 'you said you wouldn't have anyone aboard. I don't want to see anyone.'

Dinah passed Barry, and sat down across the table from Cathy. 'I came to see you,' she said, watching Cathy's face closing into rejection. 'We met last year,' she went on, and Cathy was trying not to listen. 'You were at Leo's for a week. I'm Dinah. I was downstairs, and we spent some time together.'

'Leo——' Cathy didn't want to ask. 'I wrote to him. He didn't answer.' Her voice was flat, telling Dinah she didn't care if Leo answered her letter or not.

'Your letter didn't come until a few days ago. It was mailed in February, but it didn't get to Leo's house until now.' She leaned closer, but stopped when Cathy drew back. 'Cathy, I'm sorry, but Leo died in February.'

'He never got my letter?' It took some time to sink in. Leo had not ignored her appeal. She gulped. 'I waited, went to the post office every day.'

'Honey, why didn't you phone him? You could have called collect.' The call would have come just before Leo had gone into hospital, and Leo would have done something about it, somehow got Cathy on to a plane home.

'I was scared to.' She gulped and Dinah remembered how her own fingers had trembled as she'd dialled Leo's telephone number that night ten years ago. One ring. Two. Three, and she had been starting to hang up, quickly, before he could answer.

Then his voice on the line. Her silence, fingers curling into the receiver, hurting. 'This is Leo,' he'd said for the second time. 'Who's there?'

She had managed, 'Dinah. I—You don't remember who I am.' She had been ready to hang up quickly at the slightest word from him.

'I remember,' he had said quietly, proving it by saying, 'You didn't want to go back to Prince George. I wasn't going to send you back there, Dinah.'

She had swallowed, said aggressively, 'Yeah, well. You'd have sent me somewhere, wouldn't you?'

He had not answered that, had asked, 'Where have you been?'

'Around.' She had looked out at the dark street. 'I'm fine.' A police car had slowed as it passed, the officer twisting to look into the booth. Then there had been a noise from the car radio and the flashing lights had gone on as he'd sped away. Earlier there had been the ambulance for the boy who had attacked her, and she had hidden until it had gone.

'Is that why you called me?' Leo had asked. 'To give me a line about how great everything is?'

She had been silent, her fingers tense on the receiver. Leo had asked, 'Have you had supper?'

'No.' She hadn't eaten all day.

'Then how about a meal and a bed for the night?' She realised now, looking at Cathy, how careful Leo's voice had been on the telephone that night as he'd said, 'I've got a spare room.'

'What do you want for it?' she had demanded suspiciously.

'We'll work something out.'

'I'm not going to have it on with you,' she had said sullenly.

'No,' he had agreed, and she had found herself tempted to believe that he meant it.

Leo had made a deal with her that night. She would look after his house and cook his dinners, and she could have the apartment downstairs. No restrictions on her social life, but no dope and no booze, and no noise that kept him up nights. The one condition had been that Dinah had had to agree to undergo a week of educational testing, then agree to seriously consider the resulting recommendations.

Ten years later, and Cathy's face was turning rigid with sulky rejection as she asked, 'What're you doing here? I didn't ask you to come. I don't need anyone. I'm fine.' When Cathy's eyes looked desperately around at the inside of the boat, they found Barry. Barry's going to look after me.'

Dinah wondered if Cathy could see the unease on Barry's face. She said, 'Cathy, Leo asked me to help you.' There was no sign that the girl had heard. 'There's room in the house. Leo left me the house, for me and his kids.' Leo had always called them that, his kids. Even Dinah, who was twenty-six now. 'The apartment downstairs is empty,' she said.

It had been Dinah's apartment until she'd moved upstairs after Leo died. Once she'd finished school and started working, she had paid rent. There hadn't been any reason to move. It was the only home she had. Now she said, 'There's room for you and the baby.'

'We gotta eat,' the girl said tightly. 'An' my baby's not gonna be a welfare brat like me. And don't say I can get it adopted. I'm not goin' to do that. It's my baby. I'm not giving it to anybody.'

Dinah said carefully, 'I need someone to cook supper during the weekdays, and do a bit of light housework so the house doesn't get too messy. If you wanted to do that for me, I'd give you the room and board and a bit extra. You'd have time to go back to school.'

It was almost word for word the offer Leo had made her ten years ago. Cathy unknowingly answered as Dinah had. 'I'm not much of a cook.'

'Neither am I.' Dinah relaxed a bit. 'I've got a good cookbook you can use.'

Cathy shifted uncomfortably, her hand pressing against the hard roundness of her abdomen. She looked so terribly young as she asked, 'Why school? Why do I have to do that?'

'You know the reasons. The baby. You. So you can control your own life. If that's not enough, what about Leo? You promised Leo. You said that if he helped you you'd go back to school.'

'But he didn't——'

'He sent me.' He had not said Cathy's name, but he had asked Dinah to look after the kids. 'So you've got a promise to keep.'

Cathy stared at her, her face unyielding. Outside, the wind must have shifted, coming into the bay and rocking the boat on the waves. Cathy touched her stomach gently, as if it were complaining at the motion. 'Why you? Why would he get you to look after his kids?'

'Maybe because I'm one of them.' Cathy frowned and Dinah said, 'Ten years ago it was me calling him, and he came.'

The suspicion was less, but still there. 'I'm not going to give up the baby. It's my baby.'

'That has to be your own decision,' Dinah said. Barry shifted uncomfortably, stood up as if about to leave for the cockpit outside.

'OK,' said Cathy finally, then she closed her eyes tightly and gasped painfully.

Barry said nervously, 'She's been having those pains all day. I wanted to get her to the doctor, but the weather didn't look too good and she didn't want to go.' His concern and helplessness were in his voice. He was a nice boy, knew Cathy needed help, but was not sure enough to be firm with her.

Cathy was panting slightly. 'I—I can't speak Spanish. I won't have someone looking after me who can't understand. They might do anything to me!' Cathy squeezed her eyes tight and wailed, 'I don't know anything about this! I don't know how to have a baby, and I——'

Dinah smoothed her curly red hair, but Cathy would not be calmed. She started to cry. Dinah called softly, 'Joe?'

He would know what to do. Crazy Cathy, such a baby herself, avoiding doctors, acting as if she could delay having the baby by simply saying she was not ready.

She felt Joe's hand on her shoulder and she moved aside to let him closer to Cathy. 'She needs you,' Dinah whispered.

CHAPTER NINE

JOE crouched beside Cathy as her body went rigid and she cried out in pain. His hand rested lightly on her distended abdomen.

'Oooooh! I—it hurts!'

He brushed her damp hair back, and said quietly, 'Cathy, you're fighting what's happening. Did you learn any breathing exercises for when the baby's coming?' Her head rocked back and forth in a wild negative, then her tenseness eased and she was left exhausted, her eyes closed, her face shiny with perspiration.

'Barry?' Joe's voice was a quiet command that Barry responded to instantly. 'Take my dinghy, go over to my boat—the ketch anchored just north of you. It's not locked. Go into the aft cabin and get the black leather bag that's under the chart-table seat. The seat lifts up and the bag's under, in a hatch.'

Dinah heard the engine cough as Barry pulled the cord to start it. Then it caught and she heard it roar as the dinghy sped away. Cathy was groaning, but lying quietly under Joe's touch on her shoulder. Touch is important, Leo had always said. Just a little touch, but when people are hurting it's important to let them know you're there. People like Cathy, often rejected as a child, usually shook off touches, but Joe's hand on her seemed to calm.

Dinah asked, 'Joe, what can I do?'

'See if you can find out where Barry stashes his

linen. A couple of clean sheets. A clean towel—or something to wrap the baby—Cathy, I want you to breathe slowly and deeply. That's it. You want to relax, store up your energy. Just let the breath come in and fill up your lungs very slowly, very gently. Feel yourself relaxing—Dinah, see if there aren't some tapes somewhere.'

'Tape? What for?'

'Not adhesive. Music. Something soothing to help keep her calm. There's a tape deck on the other side of the cabin. But for heaven's sake don't stick in some heavy rock!' Dinah saw Cathy grin weakly and Joe said to the girl, 'You might like it, but you don't want your baby dancing the jig, do you?'

Cathy giggled and Joe smiled as he nodded to Dinah to go searching cupboards. She found sheets in a cupboard at the back of the boat. She sorted out two white ones and brought them back to Joe, put them on the opposite settee. He was talking earnestly to Cathy in a low voice.

'That's it. When you feel . . . yes, that's the way. If you relax with it, it's easier.'

Dinah was rather amazed to find a Chopin tape. She put it in the player, and turned the volume low. Watching, she saw that the soft music did seem to have a relaxing effect on Cathy. 'Did you used to play music in the delivery room?' she asked Joe when he nodded his approval of the music.

'Depends on the hospital. Some are stodgier than others. This hospital is rather informal.'

Cathy curved her arms around her stomach. 'Joe, are you a real doctor?'

He nodded, and asked her, 'Are you from Vancouver?'

'Yes.'

'That's where I trained. If you and I had both stayed in our own country, we could have been doing this together in some hospital.' He grinned and added, 'We'd probably have a lot less fun. No music. A disapproving nurse who couldn't possibly be as pretty to look at as Dinah is.'

'No.' Cathy closed her eyes, and for a minute Dinah thought she had dropped off. 'Is it going to be all right?'

'Everything looks good.' He squeezed her hand. 'Why don't you let Dinah help you out of your things? You'll be more comfortable with just your dress and the sheet. Then when Barry gets back with my bag, I'll take a closer look. After that, we can take bets on when your daughter is going to arrive—and on whether she'll turn out to be a son.'

'She's a girl,' Cathy insisted.

It was hours before they knew the answer. Joe got Dinah to sit on a stool near Cathy's head, to talk to her and hold her hand. When Barry returned with the black bag, the two men removed the table to make an open area near Cathy. Dinah hadn't realised the table could be detached from its position, but without it there was much more room, although it couldn't be an ideal delivery-room.

Joe must have read her mind. He said, 'I thought of taking her over to our boat where there's more room, but getting her there would be an ordeal—Barry, come and sit with Cathy while Dinah and I get things ready.'

Our boat. Of course it was a slip of the tongue, but it made her heart race, her mind fill with a rush of dreams.

There wasn't really much to get ready, but it seemed to Dinah that Joe worked as hard at keeping Barry busy as he did at keeping Cathy calm. When Barry started hovering restlessly, and Joe seemed to have run out of things to send him for, Dinah asked, 'Have you figured out what to put the baby in?'

Barry shook his head worriedly, and Joe suggested, 'Why don't you and Dinah go over to my boat and look through the lazarette. I think you might find a plastic tub there that would do.'

Dinah thought Barry was relieved to be out doing something. They crossed to Joe's boat without talking, then had to look for a lantern to help them see into the lazarette. Barry lit the lantern and held it while Dinah started hauling things out.

'This lazarette hatch is a real hole,' she muttered good-naturedly. 'Ropes and cans of paint and who knows what.'

Barry was taking things as she handed them out, his mind not on what he was doing. Finally he said, 'I don't know what you must think of me. It's not—Cathy's not——' He took a deep breath, then said, 'Well, it's not my baby.'

'I know it isn't, Barry.' She leaned back on her haunches, and reached up to touch his arm fleetingly. 'Cathy needed friends. I'm glad you were here to help her.'

He nodded, and said uneasily. 'She was living on the beach. That bastard she came down here with—he just took off and left her. Dunno where he went, but she couldn't look after herself. She had nothing.'

His voice dropped and he said uneasily, 'If I could have, I'd have—I don't have a job, you see, and—this trip is something my dad gave me. I graduated last year, and he said why didn't I come down and spend a year on the boat, kind of a graduation present. My parents keep the boat down here, come for a holiday every winter. It's not that much of a boat, but it's a cheap holiday. And I didn't need much to live down here for a year. Dinah, I—when I realised Cathy had nowhere, that there was no one, just this Leo and he hadn't answered her letter—I know she needed to go to doctors and all that, and I would have if I could, would have taken her home to Canada, but honest to God I don't think my mother would have—— She just wouldn't have understood. And I didn't have the money to get her back. I'm going back next month myself, though, taking my old car back. I've got enough to eat until then, and about enough for gas money. I was gonna drive her back then, her and the baby if it came. Then—I don't know. I was going to try to help her get something worked out. I haven't got a job lined up, yet, though, and——'

Dinah pulled out a plastic mass that turned out to be a big dish pan or a small laundry tub. She held it up. 'Do you think this is it?'

He frowned. 'Is it big enough for a baby?'

'I think so. They come pretty small, you know.'

He pondered. 'Yeah,' he agreed.

Dinah started putting the rope back into the locker. 'I hope Joe doesn't mind if this stuff isn't packed the same as it was. What I really think, Barry, is that Cathy's lucky to have you for a friend.'

He made a noise like swallowing, put the plastic aside and said, 'I don't really think she should drive back, all that way with a new baby. If something goes wrong with the car I might have a problem. I don't have extra money. With just me it didn't matter. If the car packed it in I could hitch-hike, but with a baby, a new baby——'

'It's all right. I'll take her back with me.' Would it be better to send Cathy by air? But then she would arrive in Vancouver alone, and it was very important that Cathy should not feel abandoned now.

Barry seemed to be following her thoughts. 'I don't want you to think I'll just shove her off on you and—I'm gonna be in Vancouver. She'll be in Vancouver, won't she? You said she could stay at Leo's house and—yeah, well, when I get there I'll—I'll look her up. I'll get a job. I'll be stayin' at my parents, but then I'll get a job. I'll find something.' He took in a deep breath, said in a rush, 'She's pretty young, and—well, I think she should do the school thing, get herself together, but I wouldn't want her to think I walked out. I mean, she and I weren't—well, we didn't—but I'd like to come see her, and maybe take her and the baby out. To the park and stuff.' He glowered, and added, 'The school thing, too. I could help her with it, maybe.'

Dinah stood up, silencing his rush of uncomfortable words with her hand on his shoulder. 'Barry, I think she'd like that, but you should tell her yourself. Cathy hasn't had a lot of people in her life that have stuck around for her.'

He gulped, and said, 'Yeah, I know. She told me.'

If she had, then he was a closer friend than he realised. From Dinah's memories of last summer, Cathy hadn't opened up to Leo at all. Whatever was in her past had been thoroughly and painfully locked up. Dinah said simply, 'I'm glad you're her friend.' From the look on Barry's face, it was going to be more than friendship. Dinah hoped Cathy would be mature enough to realise what a good young man this was, but she said only, 'Cathy's going to need a lot of encouragement.'

'Yeah.' He took the plastic pan from her. 'Do you think we could find some soap? Soap and salt water and a cloth or something, and we could clean this thing up. I figure I could help with the school thing a lot. It's gonna be a drag for her, going back when she's been out for a couple of years. But she's smart, you know. She'll do it. And maybe——' he shrugged uncomfortably '——well, I just think I could help out a lot.'

They cleaned and dried the pan, then Dinah lined it with a big, colourful towel of Joe's. Barry smiled at it in the darkness of the boat deck and Dinah agreed that it was a pretty bassinet. They headed back to the other boat.

'Just in time,' said Joe as they came in. He looked up from Cathy, his eyes narrowing on Barry. The boy was pale. 'Barry, why don't you take a walk on the beach while——?'

'No!' Cathy gasped, and said, 'Barry, please don't leave me!'

'I won't,' said the boy, glaring at Joe who shrugged with a faint grin.

'All right, then. Sit there, hold her hand and, if you're going to faint, fall the other way.' Then Cathy cried out, and things started happening quickly. 'You're doing great,' Joe assured her, and a few moments later he was laying the tiny newborn on Cathy's stomach. 'You win,' he told the young mother. 'A girl.'

'Leonie,' whispered Cathy. 'I'm calling her Leonie, for Leo.'

After Joe had tied the cord, Cathy held the baby in her arms for a moment before she slept, then Barry took Leonie from her as if he had done this before. He flushed when his eyes met Dinah's. 'I'm from a big family,' he mumbled, rocking the newborn gently.

Joe didn't seem to need her help, nor did Cathy for that matter. Dinah went outside where only the moon would see that she was crying. Joe found her there a few moments later.

'Hi,' he said softly.

'Hi.' She sniffled a little as she turned to look at him. He touched her cheek and his fingers came away damp. She smiled tremulously, and whispered, 'I'm being silly, aren't I?'

'No.' He sat beside her in the cockpit, took her hand in his, turned it over and stared at the palm in the moonlight. 'I'd forgotten myself what a spectacular experience that is.' He said ruefully, 'Men aren't supposed to cry, but having a baby is a pretty emotional thing. We just had our first baby together.'

She licked her lips, stared at her palm as if she could see what he was reading there. His lips were turned down, his face very serious. When his eyes met hers they didn't have any of the bright blue in them, only deep black questions.

'Dinah, would you like to make a baby with me?'

She gasped, and said painfully, 'Joe—Joe, please don't—'

Then he took her other hand, too, and said, 'I didn't really mean to say that, but in there I kept having this fantasy thing, that it was you, that it was my baby.' He laughed shortly, and said, 'I never could keep any distance from this doctoring thing.'

'Joe?' It was Barry's voice. 'Joe, can you come here?'

'Yeah.' He stared down at Dinah, and she thought he was going to say something that would change her life forever. Then he shook his head, turned away, and she felt a tearing as he hurried back into the boat. Just for a moment, there had been a vision of the future, warm and wonderful. Joe and Dinah together, forever. A home. A family, his babies and hers. He had seen it too, but he was walking away and it was not going to happen.

That night she slept on the settee across from Cathy, to be near the girl and the baby, although Barry seemed to know far more than Dinah did about caring for newborn infants. But in the middle of the night she held little Leonie when she woke, and she was silly enough to dream that it was her baby, hers and Joe's.

The next morning they breakfasted together, Cathy eating very lightly on Joe's instructions, Joe announcing, 'I was talking on the radio to a boat out to the east of us, in the Gulf. The water's smooth. It looks like an easy day. I think we can head back to La Paz without disturbing Cathy or the baby too much.'

'I've been thinking about it,' said Dinah, as she pushed her eggs around on the plate, 'and I've decided that I should try to get a flight home for Cathy and me, and the baby of course. The car——' She shrugged, knowing she had to get away quickly if she was going, before she got crazy and started begging a man who didn't want her. Remembering the airline strike that had complicated her journey south, she added, 'If we can get a flight, that is.'

Everybody seemed to think that was a good idea, and Joe said, 'Don't worry about the car. If you can do without it for a while, I can see it gets back to you in Vancouver.'

'Thanks,' she said shortly. He had helped her into the country; now he seemed eager to help her out.

Booking a flight turned out to be easy as long as they were willing to drive south to Los Cabos, then fly by a circuitous route to the Mexican mainland, then north to Seattle. From Seattle they would be able to book a short flight to Vancouver. The only problem was the existence of a baby that had not entered the country. Joe managed to smooth their way through the paperwork of registering the baby's birth in Mexico, and within forty-eight hours he was driving them to the Los Cabos airport in Dinah's car.

Throughout, Joe avoided being alone with her. Their passionate union on the deck of his boat might have been a dream, for all there was in his eyes when he looked at her. All right. She had practice enough at pretending that goodbyes did not matter. She even managed to smile as he said goodbye to Cathy and Leonie at the airport. Then Barry took Cathy carefully into his arms, holding her and the baby together.

Dinah found herself staring into Joe's eyes. 'Thanks, Joe. For . . . for everything.' She managed to smile, but he did not smile back. He nodded, but he didn't hold out his hand to her, and he made no move to come closer, to take her in his arms.

His voice was husky, though, when he said, 'De nada, señorita. I'll get your car back to you.'

'No hurry. I've got Leo's old car, too, so I can use it for any camping trips with the girls. So any time—if anyone's going north and could drive it, or——' She swallowed and couldn't stop herself from saying, 'Maybe I could even come back some time, or——' She stopped before the rest of the crazy words came out.

'No. I'll look after it.' His voice was strained. Maybe it was hurting him, too, but he wasn't going to say anything but goodbye to her.

'Goodbye,' she said again, then there was the plane, and Cathy looking nervous as she settled in the seat.

Dinah had lots of time that day to prowl through her little phrase-book and translate the Spanish words Joe had said when she thanked him. De nada translated as 'it's nothing'. Nothing. He had given her almost exactly the two weeks he had promised her, and it was nothing in his life.

CHAPTER TEN

DINAH supposed she should worry about the car, but it seemed irrelevant and it wasn't that big a deal to dig out the ownership papers for Leo's old car and go down to an Autoplan office and reactivate the insurance.

It would be more inconvenient for Joe, trying to arrange her car's delivery before he left for the South Pacific on his boat. She knew that he would keep his promise, that some day her car would turn up on her doorstep, probably delivered in some unconventional manner. When it came, she thought that her tears would come with it. As long as the car was still in Mexico, she could keep having crazy fantasies that he would be the one to bring it back to her.

Jake welcomed her back to work with a stack of assignments that had her staying late, and taking work home at weekends. It seemed that Austin Media swallowed her whole for a while, with only moments to show Cathy how to cook an omelette and how not to burn steaks, to make sure the girl got to the college for testing and to the public health unit for a long talk with the nurse. Sally, one of the girls Dinah regularly took out camping, turned out to have a passion for babies and quite a bit of practical knowledge about their care.

Then Barry turned up, and he had no idea where Joe might be or what had happened to Dinah's car. Barry was still dark from the sun, but within days he started looking more Canadian—he even turned up one day in a suit, on his way to a job interview. Dinah watched the slow growth of the relationship between Cathy and Barry. Both youngsters seemed cautious, which seemed to Dinah a good thing. They were so terribly young.

Dinah's dreams became less optimistic, more filled with a yearning that she tried to bury in busy days. She started watching her mailbox, hoping for a letter from Joe about her car, or at least a postcard. She knew that if a letter came he would not sign it with love, would not be begging her to join him in some crazy corner of the world.

She would go. If he asked, she would go, and if he was there, loving her, she thought that she could make a home anywhere, that a house would not matter.

Perhaps he had written, but it was buried somewhere in the mail system that had tried to digest Cathy's letter to Leo. Perhaps. But if there was a letter somewhere, it was not a message of love. She knew better. Darn it, wasn't she a practical girl, a realist? Not a dreamer, for goodness' sake. Dreamers just got slapped in the face.

She tried to finish a painting of Cathy's baby, but somehow painting seemed impossible. Nothing looked good. The commercial drawings she did at work were easier. Thank goodness she hadn't lost that skill, or she'd have to worry about going hungry! Especially after all the travelling, airline tickets, and most recently the furniture bill for a baby crib and washstand.

In late July she decided to clean out Leo's store-room. It was a job she had been avoiding for months. Leo had filled the room with a pile of old junk he hadn't wanted to get rid of over the years.

None of it was of any value, and there didn't seem to be much of sentimental value as far as she could see. Leo hadn't been a man for photo albums or mementos from the kids he helped. He'd just been there, helping them.

If he had had family of his own, there was no sign in this room. She'd wondered if getting into this store-room would uncover some hidden life of Leo's. Once he had told her that his only relative was a third cousin he hadn't seen in over twenty years, and his act of leaving everything to Dinah seemed to confirm that.

Certainly there were no family mementos in the junk-room, but by noon she had discovered there was a lot of dirt. There were also five pairs of ice-skates in assorted sizes, two sleeping-bags, and three boxes of parts for an electric train set. Maybe she wouldn't use the room as a studio after all. The sun-room at the back of the house was working well enough, and perhaps it would be fun to try to reconstruct this massive electric train thing. The girls might get a kick out of that. She would save it for a rainy weekend when the camping trip looked a dismal prospect, then bring them all over here. They could build trains, or try to, and laugh over their childish pursuits.

She was thinking of stopping for a cup of coffee when the doorbell rang. Earlier Cathy had come upstairs with Barry and the baby, but they had left quickly before she could involve them in what looked like a dirty, hard-working task. Now, sitting back on her heels with a little train engine in her hands, she realised that she was a bit dizzy. She must have forgotten to have breakfast again.

She pushed at a stray clump of hair with the back of her hand. The doorbell rang again. 'Coming!' she shouted. 'Just hold on!' If it was Cathy, she'd just walk in. Jake and his wife Jenny might come for a Saturday visit, but they'd open the door and shout in when she didn't answer. So it was probably that fellow next door who kept complaining she was feeding his cat. Darn! She'd meant to stop feeding the furry thing, but it kept coming, meowing, and not understanding why Dinah wouldn't give it milk any more.

'How the devil does he know I'm feeding it?' she muttered, as she went down the corridor. She felt another clump of hair working its way out of the knot she'd tried to restrain it with. Impatiently, she reached up and pulled out a couple of pins, letting it free. Maybe she'd go to the hairdresser's and get it cut, short. When would she stop remembering the feel of Joe's hands in it, his breath stirring the soft hair against her cheek?

'OK!' she shouted. He was impatient, angry probably. She jerked the door open. 'Look, I'm sorry about your cat, but——'

His fair hair was brushed smooth, glistening and tidy. He was clean-shaven except for the moustache which seemed to have been trimmed since she'd last seen it. She swallowed, realised her mouth was open, and got it closed.

'I don't have a cat,' he said, not smiling. 'Hello, señorita.'

'You're—you're wearing a suit.' It was a silly thing to say, but all the other things, the questions and the heart-stopping joy, were unspeakable until she knew why he was here, at her door, not looking like the Joe she knew.

He nodded, shifted from one foot to the other and slipped his hands into his pockets. 'Can't go to an interview in jeans. Not if you care about the result.'

'Interview?' Was it possible that he was nervous? Joe? 'Are you going to come in?' She stepped back and he didn't answer, but he came through the door. Inside, the two of them standing there, the silence was no more comfortable. 'What—Joe, why are you here?'

He shifted, looked at a painting that had been done by one of her girls. He frowned and she wanted to tell him she was keeping it because she loved Sally, not because she had weird taste in art.

'I brought your car back.' He slid his right hand out of that pocket and the keys were in his hand. He held them out.

Her fingers closed on them, her heart sinking. The car. 'Of course. You said you'd get it back to me. I—I didn't know you meant you'd bring it.' She swallowed. 'Where's the boat?'

'Mexico.' He looked so temporary, uncomfortable in the suit, uneasy, as if he were leaving as soon as he could. 'San Carlos,' he added.

'I thought you were going to——Where's San Carlos?'

'There's more than one San Carlos, but this one is across the Sea of Cortez, on the mainland side. Further north.' She nodded. He was going back, of course. His boat was there and he had come north to bring the car, not to see Dinah. If he asked, she would go with him, but he was not going to ask. Just as well, she supposed, because loving would be mixed with the old terrors of being homeless, never knowing where tomorrow would leave her. And anyway, how could she abandon Leo's kids?

He was explaining about some marina where his boat could be left in bond while he left the country. 'Interview?' she asked again. 'What interview?' She swallowed, and said, 'Coffee? Do you want some coffee? I was just going to make some. Or a drink? Or—'

He shook his head. She bit her lip. So he was not going to stay long enough even for a drink.

He shifted his balance from one foot to the other, half leaned against the wall, then straightened. He wasn't comfortable, probably wanted to be gone. He asked, 'How's Cathy? And the baby?'

'I—Cathy's out. With Barry.' She found herself chattering on, her voice sounding almost as nervous as she felt. 'They've gone to Stanley Park. Barry has this theory that the baby should have sun, and that Cathy can study better outside. Cathy's doing upgrading courses at the community college. Then she's going to take a computer course.'

'Good,' he said absently. Was he listening?

'Barry's got a job. With the City. He's starting next week.' She added desperately, 'If you'd like to see them, they'll be back in an hour or two.' She rubbed her hands along the denim fabric over her thighs. 'You could stay, wait.' She was probably crazy. Two hours of this awkward non-communication and she'd be up the wall.

His shoulders shifted in the jacket, his hands dug deeper in the trousers. 'I—ah—' He broke off and walked past her, to the window, prowling his way across the living-room as if he needed to be free.

'Where are you staying?' she asked his back.

'My brother.' He picked up a big seashell that was not particularly pretty, turned it in his hand. 'I got in yesterday.'

'Oh.' So he hadn't been in a hurry to see her. Obviously, because he didn't even want to be here. It was a duty. He'd wanted to see the baby, of course. He'd delivered it, and must have a special interest in it for that. She remembered how moved he had been by the birth. 'I—how long are you here for?' Maybe it was only the car. A promise to be kept, delivering it. 'Couldn't you find anyone to drive the car up?'

'I didn't look.' He swung around and she winced as his shoulder just missed a glass pitcher standing on the bookcase. 'You said you could get by without it.'

He was watching her hands try to rub a hole in the fabric of her jeans. She said desperately, 'Are you sure you won't have a cup of coffee? I'll make some.' She dashed away to make it, not waiting for an answer.

Coward, escaping to the kitchen. She'd dreamed that he would come, not believed it. Now she was spilling coffee grounds all over the counter, afraid to go back out there because if she said what she really wanted he would look uncomfortable, trapped, and he'd be gone.

It was a relief to hear the laughter out front, the door and sounds of Cathy and Barry. When Dinah brought the coffee out, Cathy was describing the horrors of learning algebra to Joe, while Joe sat on the footstool, holding the baby and rocking it gently as he listened.

'She'll learn,' Barry said to Joe, and Cathy claimed that Barry was terrorising her into being a mathematician.

'We were just going to make dinner,' said Barry. Recently, he had taken over teaching Cathy to cook. 'Dinah, what do you think about liver and onions?'

Cathy groaned and Joe said, 'I was going to take Dinah out for dinner.'

'Smart,' said Cathy. 'Can I come? I hate liver.'

'It's good for you,' said Barry, and that seemed to settle Cathy's ambitions for a night out.

That left Joe looking at Dinah, and she realised he must be expecting an answer, although he hadn't actually asked her to go out. It was probably just a way of getting out of the liver.

'I'll just wash up,' she said quickly, before he could change his mind. 'Should I change?'

'It doesn't matter.'

Oh, lord! This was going to hurt. 'I'll change,' she decided, because it would give her time to get herself together. 'I'm not a match for your suit.'

'Wear the black dress,' suggested Cathy. 'It's super!'

She had a shower, tried three dresses on and discarded them all. The black was too slinky, as if she was inviting him to want her. Would he? There was no desire in his eyes, and she was afraid to make a bid for his interest in her as a woman. Surely he remembered, though? Hadn't that explosion of their loving shaken him, too? Just once, and she was never going to forget it. If he took her again, held out his arms and opened his lips, she would be clinging, begging, when he was fighting to be free of her.

Not the white dress either. It was too young, too vulnerable, and if her hand trembled it would show where she spilled her food on it. Somehow she had to get through this evening, keep her cool and not make him feel that she was someone he would run halfway around the world to avoid. If he wanted to go out, he wanted a pleasant evening. Not a clinging limpet.

If he wanted loving, wouldn't there be something in his eyes besides that hard blue? So she mustn't tell him again, must not say the words of love that welled up inside her when she met his eyes.

She jumped, hearing a sound like a door closing. Panicked, she called out, 'Joe? I'll be just a second! I'm almost ready!'

The blue. It was light and swirly, but modest with a high neck and a very plain bodice over the full skirt. It had to be the blue. There was no more time to fiddle around with deciding. And he liked her in blue, didn't he? She had worn blue the day they had made love.

Joe almost left when she went to change. What was the point? A rotten evening, fighting his desire to take her in his arms, to touch her face and see her eyes take fire . . . to tell her his dream of the future and see her eyes go cold. Ever since she had opened the door to him, it had been obvious. Whatever had happened on the deck of a boat, whatever impulsive words of love she had declared rashly in a far-off foreign country, back here at home it was different.

After Cathy and Barry had taken the baby downstairs, Joe had gone to the front door, opened it softly, but it was no use. She was in his heart, and it would not change for walking away. He closed the door, heard her call out something about being almost ready. While he waited he prowled the house. It was filled with signs of the girls she spent so much of her time with. Young girls like Cathy, who needed someone and were afraid to reach out.

As Dinah had been.

But she had been his, in his arms, closer in his heart than anyone had ever been. Even Julie. Julie was so far back, so sweet and painful both at once. He had loved her, but there had never been this wild meeting of souls, as if he and Dinah had been together forever in some other time, some other dimension, as if when they touched there was nothing that could part them, not heart or soul or flesh.

It must have frightened Dinah, being that close, that vulnerable, that wide open to another person. It had scared hell out of him, he knew, had turned his world upside down.

In the end, it had made sense out of life again. That was what she had done for him, but maybe it wasn't so simple for her. She needed time. All right. He could give her that. If a kid like Barry could take time to be patient with Cathy, then surely he could be patient too? He was a man, more mature and . . .

And he wanted her, needed her in his life with an ache that threatened to turn him into a helpless fool. He had to do better than that. It might take time. Weeks. Months. But where the hell did he start? It might take years. He swallowed and tried to believe he could be patient enough not to mess it up, not to rush her. Dinner dates first. Talk. There must be something they could talk about, some way to relax this explosive tension he felt without frightening her into slamming that door and shutting him out of her home and her life.

Not for touching, he thought wryly, when she came out in the blue dress with that bright smile on her face. All right. He could wait, could court her again, slowly. So he started with talking, spending the drive to the restaurant asking her about her work, about the paintings she had been working on. She didn't want to talk about her hopes for an exhibition of her paintings, it seemed, so over dinner he talked about the interview he had been to that day.

She listened, trying to know what it was in his

eyes, why he was so uncomfortable with her.

He spread his hands on the table, seemed to change his words as they started coming out. 'It's not—well, the job's not that much money. But it's something I've been interested in. Dr Mul—he was one of my professors when I was in medical school, and later we saw each other and—then Hank was telling me a couple of months ago that Dr Muldern had been talking to him. They'd run into each other at one of these Medical Association things.' She nodded as if she knew what he meant and he said, 'Somehow they got on to me as a topic, I guess because Hank is Dr Mitchell too, and so am I. Dr Muldern told Hank that if I ever contemplated going back into medicine, he'd like to talk to me about getting into research.'

'So you did? I mean, talk to him?' Joe was being surprisingly unclear. It wasn't like him to ramble on and not get to the point. 'And you're going to?' she prodded him. 'You'll be working with this doctor. That's good, isn't it? I mean, you're happy about it, aren't you?' He didn't look happy.

'Yeah. It's OK. I—well, I've really been thinking about coming back, but I can't see me getting into general practice again. And it's not as if I'm needed there. Canada's not short of doctors, and—well, I don't know if I'll ever be ready to go back to practising. You've got to keep a distance from the patients, got to be able to roll with it when you lose them. Of course, a good doctor cares, but—well, it shouldn't take him apart. The research—it's important, I think, and I believe I can do a good job. Dr Muldern thinks so, or he wouldn't have made the proposal. But—well, Dinah, it's not the same thing as an economic proposition.'

'Why not?' What the devil was he talking about?

'The pay isn't good. I'll be half a student and half a worker for quite a while. I've got a lot to learn. Some day I might get tenure at the university, but if that doesn't happen there might never be that much security in it. It's just a job I want to do.'

'The security doesn't matter that much to you, does it?' She frowned. Was she missing something, or was he simply not making sense? 'I mean, if you could roam around on a boat, living on a shoestring. Well, it—is it here? In Vancouver? At the university here?' He nodded and her voice rushed on, saying, 'Then, why don't you move in with me? There's lots of room and it would be cheaper for you and——'

Her words were echoing around the table. Something had happened to his face, his eyes, and she was scared when she heard her own words coming back to her. 'Oh, God!' she whispered. 'Joe, I—I don't believe I said that. I . . .' Of course he didn't want that. Dinner, he'd said, and she'd begun to hope he might dance with her later when that band got their notes smoothed out a bit. 'Your brother, you said, didn't you? Of course, you're going to live with your brother.'

'I don't think so.' His voice sounded so odd, so . . . 'He's way out in Surrey, and—Dinah——'

'I know,' she said hurriedly, her hand fluttering towards his, drawing back sharply. 'I—I didn't really mean . . .'

Living together. Waking him up in the morning if he slept in, going to sleep knowing he was there. She would put him in the next room, and if he turned in the bed she would hear. Making dinner, knowing he was coming, or even coming home and finding him there before her, the smell of dinner on the air. Loving. Making love. Talking. Watching television together, laughing about the bad acting in a film. She gulped back tears, and said desperately, 'You'll get your own place, of course. I—I just meant if . . .'

She closed her eyes. It wasn't going to get better. She wasn't going to be able to talk her way out of it, not with his eyes watching, seeing too much. She wailed, 'Joe, I have to get out of here. Please. I—I don't think I can handle any more of this evening. I—I thought I could do it and pretend—I—I'm sorry, but I just can't.' Oh, God! She was going to cry, really cry. She pushed her chair back and heard it make a loud noise. 'I—excuse me!'

She ran, stumbling around a woman at the next table, running headlong past the waiter and through a door. She pushed the door shut behind herself, leaning back against it and feeling the tears coming. With the door shut it didn't matter if she cried. She had the whole shiny washroom to herself.

She had never been a coward. She'd been reckless, running away when staying would have been better, striking out at that boy on the beach when it might have made things worse, going off to Baja without stopping to think and prepare enough. But she'd always faced things when there was no way out.

So how did she end up here? Mopping up tears in the washroom and wondering how long she would have to stay in here for him to be gone when she came out. She loved him. Maybe she'd loved him from that moment when he'd talked English to her up on a mountain in Mexico, certainly from the time he'd first kissed her. Of course she wasn't very good at loving, didn't have a lot of practice, and she sure didn't know how you went about a dinner date with a man you loved when he didn't really seem to want the loving. After all, she had told him she loved him once already, back there in Mexico, and if he wanted it . . .

Fool! Blurting out an invitation for him to move in with her. What a position for a man to be in, having to say no, thanks, but I don't want to live with you.

With cold water and a paper towel she managed to get her face looking reasonable. She'd left her bag back at the table, so she couldn't do anything about the lipstick that was gone, the mascara that had run and was washed away now. If she went back out there he probably wouldn't eat her. If he laughed, she would die, but he wasn't going to do that. He might feel sorry for her. She hoped not.

She gnawed on her lips. OK, so it would be awful. She would just have to manage it. If she got out a spurt of bright conversation quickly, he'd probably help her make it seem normal. The alternative was to stay in here forever. She took a deep breath, checked that she didn't look too bad in the mirror. Pale. Well, there was no way she could pretend she didn't care now. If it showed on her face, that was too bad. She'd get through this evening somehow, and then it wouldn't matter. She would never see him again.

He was waiting for her just outside the washroom door. He took her arm and handed her bag to her. She didn't look at his eyes, and thank heaven he didn't say anything about the scene she'd been making.

'What about the boat?' she asked brightly, as he walked her past the cashier and out of the door. No one was shouting at him, so he must have already paid the bill. 'What about Alice?' she added nervously. 'If you're going to do research, you're not going to the South Pacific, are you?'

He was making it hard work for her, his face stiff and angry. Surely he could co-operate with this small-talk business? 'What about Alice? Did you just leave her there on the beach?' She had a horrible thought and gulped out, 'She's not here with you, is she?'

His fingers bit into her arm as he leaned to put the key into the passenger door of her car. 'Alice is on a Fisher thirty,' he ground out, jerking the door open.

'A what? Fishing what?' She stared at the seat. He was waiting for her to get in, but she wasn't ready to be shut up in her car with him. She had been wrong. She simply couldn't handle this.

'A Fisher thirty. It's a sailboat. Couple on it going to Australia.' His voice was fast and angry. 'Alice is crewing to Tahiti with them. That's where she wanted to get and—— Damn it, Dinah! I don't want to talk about Alice. Will you get in the bloody car?'

She got in. Then he got in, sat there with the keys in his hand and just stared through the window. She pleated her skirt with her fingers, and decided it was time she stopped being such a coward.

'Look, Joe, I——'

'Dinah, I wish I knew what the hell you want.' He turned to glare at her and she found herself drawing back because he seemed to fill the space all around.

'What I want?' She couldn't breathe. Coward, she thought. Tell him. But didn't he know?

'Conversation?' He sounded bitter. He raked his hand through his hair and it stopped looking tidy. 'I'm having a hell of a time with conversation, but I'll try.' He faced the windscreen again, and jammed the key into the ignition.